THE BULL

THE BULL

BOOK ONE

JOHN STONE

Kenmore, WA

For more information visit www.fannypress.com

This is a work of fiction. Names, characters, places, brands, media, and incidents are either the product of the author's imagination or are used fictitiously.

The Bull
Copyright © 2022 by John Stone

ISBN: 978-1-684920-65-5 (Trade Paper)
ISBN: 978-1-684920-66-2 (eBook)

Library of Congress Control Number: 2022936010

Printed in the United States of America

For Serema. I write because she no longer can.

1

"SHOW ME WHAT HE LOOKS LIKE AGAIN," I asked my wife. She held up her phone and I saw, once again, a picture of a handsome dark-haired man. His classic features were enhanced by a three-day growth of beard and a slightly crooked smile. The most startling aspect of it was the dark, deep-set eyes that seemed to leap off the 5G screen, peering into my soul in high resolution. Knowing without being told, my most hidden desires. Things I had never admitted to myself. As I stared, the handsome man's unmoving visage seemed to say," I know what you two need, and you are about to get it."

We wandered toward the back of the dark crowded bar, my attention still fixated on the phone pic, when with her free hand she pointed toward a corner table. Sitting there, alone, was the man in the picture. The man whom she hoped would fulfill her dreams. The man I hoped would not make all my nightmares come true.

Diane and I had been married for almost three years and she had been sexually frustrated the entire time. Before though she would have never admitted as much. Our union was the result of a short affair that ended my 23-year marriage. The affair was then followed by a courtship that resulted in a hasty marriage. The whole process took six months.

At 52 years old I'd been flattered beyond belief by the attentions of the gorgeous 37-year-old attorney who was handling some details of the liquidation of my parents' estate. My mother had passed months earlier, a year after my father. My three kids were all off at college, leaving Elizabeth, my wife then, and I alone. Slowly, I drifted away, unmoored. Until in my wake, I found Diane, beautiful and blonde. Possessed of classic features and a body showing the effects of hours of gym time and no childbearing, she was kind and attentive and yet always behaved professionally. Well not all times, but any improprieties took place at the end of the process and had no bearing on the estate and its resolution. Once our romance began, I was hooked. Diane pointed me to an attorney at her firm who specialized in divorce and the whole process took less time than it should have given our marital assets. Elizabeth was gracious and understanding, and ready to get out of what had become a sleepwalk marriage.

She got a generous settlement and flew to Lucerne, and I got Diane.

Despite however flattered, I might have been, I tried hard not to kid myself. Though I worked to stay in decent shape, I was a moderately attractive male who, if he was a mid-level, IT guy wouldn't have ever had a shot with a woman as hot as Diane. Deep down I knew why she married me. Adding to the stinging realization was the fact I was under-endowed and had performance anxiety because of it. I could however take comfort in the fact that I had not been chosen by this incredible woman for the size of my dick. The size of my portfolio had always made up for a lot and it did again with the woman I adored more than life itself.

Not to say that those factors didn't create problems. They were a source of frustration for her and therefore a source of anxiety for me. I merely tried to pretend it didn't matter while I knew it did and bought her another bauble. Finally, after several drawers full of expensive jewelry and no orgasms not produced by either my tongue or her Hitachi Wand, Diane set out on an exploration of sexual discovery. Not to cheat, she never cheated, never went behind my back. I was afraid of that, and she assured me she still loved me very much, but we needed to add to our marriage as she wasn't unfulfilled and angry. First, we tried swinging and swapping, joining a website dedicated to that purpose. We attended some gatherings, but, difficult as it might be to understand, wives don't like to swap a fully functioning husband for one with a small undependable dick. So, after a few failed attempts, we decided swinging might not be for us.

That's when Diane came upon what she decided was the answer to our marital woes. The Hot wife phenomenon. Together we could find suitable men and she could have all the sex she wanted, and I'd be involved. I had discovered through swinging that I was not plagued by the jealousy attendant to most husbands. I wanted her happy and fulfilled and I liked to watch. Her porn star body was beautiful to me and the few times we had gone to swinging parties, I ended up sitting with a glass of whatever we had brought along (most were BYOB), as whatever middle-aged man with a bit of a gut, with a cock not a lot bigger than mine but in better working order, fucked my wife's brains out. As it was explained to me, Hot wifing allowed us to pick and choose from numerous attractive, well-hung men, all local or semi-local. After weeks of spending more time on the internet scanning websites devoted to this practice than she was writing legal briefs, she found him. The one we would finally meet, and interview. Dan.

At 40, "Dan the man" was 15 years younger than my then age of 55 and the same age as Diane. That birthday had been a source of tremendous angst for her when it occurred, and I wondered if the room I had reserved for our friends and family at a swanky local restaurant should be draped in black crepe. However, finding that a hunky guy like Dan was the same age renewed her faith in the vitality of her age. She told me looking at Dan's bio on the computer screen, life begins at 40, right?

As I read, I realized he was the only less than me, in terms of age. If the information was accurate, at 6 feet 3 inches, he was seven inches taller than me. At 205 pounds he was 15 pounds heavier, but his body contours indicated the difference was all muscle. His "endowment," was listed as nine inches which, compared to mine was, well, MORE. I looked at the number twice and decided it had to be an exaggeration. Most men lied about the size of their dicks. In fact, I recalled telling one girl I wanted to have sex with that mine was six inches. Her reaction once we were in bed was "Aww," which made me sense she was disappointed. Deep down I hoped if it ever came to that point, Diane's reaction to seeing Dan's would be, "Aww."

2

"**I** think that's him," she said leaning toward me till her golden blonde hair fell on my shoulder and I could feel her breath on my neck as she spoke. I nodded in agreement. "My God, he's big," she whispered in an impressed tone. I nodded again, unable to speak, or fully express what I recognized later was a welling fear mingled with a large dose of excitement. He sprawled rather than sat, spreading out and taking up most of the space around him. He saw us but waited until we got very close before he sprang with an effortless grace from his chair to say hello, warmly greeting Diane while barely acknowledging me.

"You must be Diane," he said and looking briefly toward me, added, "Jack, right?" I nodded again and offered my hand. An offer that was ignored.

"I'm Dan," then he gestured toward the table. "Let's sit." When we started to sit in chairs across the table from where he had been, he waved us off, like an air traffic controller.

"You sit there, Jake," he said hesitating slightly before getting my name wrong while pointing at one of the chairs on the far side of the table and taking Diane's hand and guiding her to the chair next to him, which he pulled close. To my surprise, my normally strong-willed independent wife took the guidance and sat, meekly, lowering herself into the seat while gazing at Dan in apparent fascination. As I sat seeing and not believing the sight of my wife holding hands with this younger, bigger, more handsome man, the table and their attitudes created space between us, the waiter approached and startled me, and I jumped slightly. Dan laughed and as a result, Diane laughed, embarrassing me, which was his point. He followed it up asking her, "Is he always so timid?" Laughing more, my wife looked at me thoughtfully, and replied, "Yes, he is now that you mention it." They laughed together, much to my discomfort, after which Dan remarked. "Like a little rabbit." More laughter only interrupted by the waiter taking our drink order.

"I'll have a Johnny Blue," Dan told the young man. "She'll have a Vodka Collins. Make it a double." I was slack-jawed as she smiled at him. Never in the three years, we'd been together had I presumed to order for her, and if I had, she would have gotten something else just to spite me. His doing it only made her smile in an amused fashion and nod. Finally, the waiter asked me what I wanted, and I ordered Irish Whiskey.

"They make a mean 'Pink lady' here. Or so I'm told," Dan said teasingly. Diane laughed at his joke much more than made me comfortable, but little did I know that would be a high point of my comfort with the conversation. We sat silently for several minutes with Dan holding my wife's hand until he finally spoke.

"So, Diane tells me you're impotent?" The tactless comment caused Diane to gasp and me to stare stunned as the drinks came. Dan shrugged and thanked our server who spun on his heel to depart the awkward scene.

"What?" He asked, drawing out the word into four syllables. Diane shook her head but was grinning as she did it and did not let go of his hand. I sat stoically not knowing what to say. Dan took that as a reason to continue, so he did.

"It's vital we all be very honest about things in this," He explained. "If this is going to work." That made sense, so this time I was the one who nodded. Diane squeezed his hand and nodded as well as saying that she agreed.

"The thing is," Dan said as he resumed holding court, "there's no need to be ashamed."

The big man took a sip of his drink as Diane and I listened silently, which was the reaction he sought to cultivate.

"We all have things we can do and things we cannot do," He continued. "You can't fuck, I can. This lady deserves it and more than that, desperately needs it. It's why we are here." I took a sip and if I had expected to see my wife bristle at being characterized as desperate, I would have been sadly disappointed. She smiled and looked at him adoringly, while carefully ignoring me. I took a larger sip and kept listening. What he said next shocked me. Letting go of her hand, he directed it under the table.

"Diane," he said with a quiet authority, "Put your hand between my legs."

Looking uncertain, she hesitated, and he said, very firmly. "Do it."

I shook my head slightly as I saw her shoulder move slightly and then I heard her giggle. Dan smirked and brought her hand back above the table and held it again.

"Tell your husband," He commanded. Diane giggled again.

"He . . . he's HUGE!" As she said it her voice took on an amazed tone and her eye glowed. Seeing that happen in front of me made me drain my glass, a fact noted by the huge dark-haired man.

"You finished your drink I see," he said in an amused tone. He then looked at Diane's, which had barely a sip out of it. "You swallow well," was his comment. "I'll have to teach that skill to your wife, won't I?"

Then, ignoring whether I replied or not he waved to our waiter and ordered another round.

3

DAN CONTINUED TALKING AND I CONTINUED LISTENING as Diane clung tightly to his hand. I was unsure if she heard a thing he said, which was amazing to me in that she was trained in a profession where listening was at a premium. She gazed as Dan adoringly as though spellbound, through three drinks. Finally, Dan declared it time for dinner, and he paid the check and we adjourned to the dining room, where his behavior towards Diane further muddied the relationship waters, as quickly the waitstaff thought he was her husband, a misperception he seemed to encourage, and which, when I started to correct it, produced a dirty look from my wife.

Again, Diane was seated beside Dan, with me on the other side of the table. The waiter came by with a menu and Dan ordered another round of drinks and asked for the wine list. Looking at it, he placed it back on the table. Looking up, he smiled. What was becoming clear was, he was making the decisions, and our opinions might be considered, but might also be ignored. That fact, along with his attitude was making me uneasy. The waiter came back and brought our drinks and took our food orders. I was once again startled when, after Dan ordered the Porterhouse and I ordered the

Filet (The petite filet as Dan pointed out mockingly), then Diane, usually averse to eating beef, ordered the Porterhouse as well.

"I'm starved for a huge hunk of meat." She said as she gave Dan a sidelong glance, smiling. The remark made him laugh.

"That's what happens when you spend years on a diet of cocktail weenies," he commented, his dark eyes looking directly at me. I winced and wasn't sure if it was the cruelty of the remark or the power of his eyes. Whichever it was, Dan noticed my reaction and laughed. To my dismay, so did my wife. They were still chuckling and moving closer to each other as the sommelier brought the wine.

Dinner was served and consumed. I noticed Dan was becoming more "familiar" with Diane. Not leering so much as closely examining her in ways you do not expect to have happen with another man regarding your wife. He was looking at her the way someone looks at a fine and expensive car they are considering for purchase. Diane noticed too, and what I observed was not the reaction I expected from her, based on previous experience. She wasn't insulted at being objectified. She was flattered. She was being seduced by his obvious misogyny and more than that, his subtle abuse of me, her husband, as Dan asserted his position as the Alpha Male at this table. The question that began to form, at the back of my brain was, given these facts, how could I let this continue? We had met this man in hopes he could be a sexual partner for Diane. Given what I'd observed, given what I feared, how could I let this extend beyond a casual meeting in a public place?

We had finished our meals, dessert, and coffee and looked across the table at my two dinner companions and they were kissing. A deep, probing passionately intrusive kiss that caused other patrons to stop and look despite themselves. I knew that because it stopped me, and I looked, wondering what had gone wrong with the simple meeting Diane and I had planned. The final evidence of my total loss of control was when, after, at long last, the kiss broke off, my wife looked into the dark eyes of this other man whom she had just met and said, "Shall we adjourn to our house for . . . drinks?"

4

Trying to follow Dan's nimble sports car through the busy suburban streets was difficult. The fact that he was going 20 miles over the speed limit made it almost impossible. Even though I knew where we were going. He knew too, because Diane volunteered to ride with him, so he "wouldn't get lost." My fear wasn't him getting lost, it was that he would turn over the small car while driving too fast and groping my wife. Finally, our street was up ahead, and I heard Dan's tires squeal as he made the turn. Three of our neighbors heard it too and I saw them looking out their windows as the supercharged sports car came to a skidding stop in our drive and the tall, dark, handsome man, and my wife leaped out of the car and ran arm in arm toward the front door. I looked toward them and waved in an embarrassed fashion as I brought up the rear. Only one waved back.

Once I got in the house, I realized Dan and Diane were already in the living room conversation pit, and what they were doing was not conversation. They were instead locked in a passionate embrace and kissing. Back when I was in high school, I would have described the behavior as "necking." This was a different time, and I was way too mature to use terms like that. Tonsil hockey or tongue fucking seemed a more accurate description. When they finally came up for air, Diane threw her head back and made an exclamation that employed no discernible words, only sounds that seemed primal. Meanwhile, Dan coolly looked over at me, smiled, and said, "I'll take a Scotch, light ice. Diane said you have Johnny Blue. That will be fine." Having placed his order, he turned back to my wife, who was after all was his primary focus and they resumed their kiss, separating only long enough for him to tell me to, "Bring my beautiful girl here a vodka. Straight up, with a twist."

Going to the bar area, I tried to understand what had happened. Unable to produce an acceptable answer, I began to make the drinks. Dan's Scotch with light ice, Diane's Vodka with a twist. Having put theirs together, I pulled out another tumbler and poured it half full of Johnny Blue. Looking out toward the seating area, I slammed the whisky, and, picking up their glasses, I headed to where a man I barely knew was becoming intimately acquainted with my wife's bridgework.

I watched as I stood holding their drinks and waiting for them to take a breath. Finally, my patience gave out, and placed both glasses on the coffee table at the center of the room, and walked back to the bar, settling myself on a stool, and finished the last of the Blue I'd poured for myself. Finally, I got tired of hearing the low moans and slurping sounds coming from my living room and got off my perch on the barstool and went to turn on some music. The old jazz Diane loved so much. As I listened my mind went back, to a happier time, when Diane and I had danced to this same song. Happier for me at least. My wife on the other hand seemed pretty God damned happy sucking face with a man who she didn't know till three hours earlier.

Then after what seemed like a very long time, I heard Diane's voice. "Jack, can you bring us fresh drinks?"

Relieved that they finally separated enough so she could speak, I put together a fresh Scotch for him and vodka for her, carefully carving off the twist. Looking at the small knife, I thought back several minutes to when I wondered if I wanted to use it to slit my wrists. I picked up the two glasses and headed to the living room, confident, we would now sit down and talk all this out like adults. Until that is, Diane rushed past me dragging Dan behind her. As she hurried down the long hall my wife yelled back at me. "Bring the drinks to the bedroom, okay?"

I watched as the pair ran down the hall to my bedroom and slammed the door. Following their path though much more slowly, I tried the knob. It was locked. I stood there holding the two drinks as I heard frantic activity behind the locked door, realizing I had two alternatives. Take the glasses and dump them in the bar sink. I could pretend I was preserving some shred of my dignity by sitting on a barstool while a man was fucking my wife's brains out in my own bedroom. In my own home, on my own bed. Having done that, I will have denied him of his drink.

I didn't do that. I did what any thoughtful husband would do in that circumstance. I put one of the drinks on the floor beside the door and knocked. When there was no response, knocked again, and the frenzied noise slowed, and I picked up the other drink and was holding it when a pants less Dan opened the door. Wide enough I could see my now naked wife sitting up on the bed, clutching the sheet to her breasts as though I hadn't been seeing them on a regular basis for three and a half years. As I handed Dan the drinks, I tried not to look. I really did. Resisting the urge to see the source of Diane's delight was too much. She had been right when she did her palpation in the bar. It really was huge. Taking the drinks, Dan realized I was staring, and his mouth formed a wide, satisfied mile.

"Sorry I can't invite you in," He said, smirking, "we're kinda busy."

With that, he closed the door in my face, and I heard the click of the lock. So, I did what I should have done, to begin with. Went to the bar, sat on a stool, and decided to drink enough to help me pretend I still had any self-esteem left. As the wild, animalistic purely sexual sounds drifted through the quiet house I knew there wasn't enough scotch in the world to do that.

Finally, when it was very late and I was very drunk, and the sexual cacophony had quieted in my bedroom, I staggered down the hall and pressed my ear to the door, on the other side of which, I could hear snoring. In three and a half years I had never known Diane to snore, so through deductive reasoning, I knew Dan was sleeping. A combination of scotch and post-coital languor. Probably my wife too. So faced with another decision I decided to go the path of least resistance. As satisfying as the idea of throwing him out onto the lawn might be in the abstract, it was only going to give the neighbors more to look at. So instead, I went to the hall bathroom, relieved myself, then repaired to one of the two spare bedrooms. The one set up for company, not the one I used as an at-home office. Once inside, I closed and locked the door. I pulled off my suit coat and laid it across a straight-backed chair. I kicked off my shoes and unbuckled my belt, dropping my slacks and laying them neatly on the chair with my coat. Finally, I unbuttoned my shirt and left it with the rest of my clothes and in my boxers and socks, turned back the bedcovers, and climbed in. I drifted off into an uneasy sleep. Later in the night, more sounds began in the other room which woke me. As I listened, I realized something. I was erect. My cock, though still small, was rock hard. Reaching in, I pulled it out of my shorts, through the fly, and began to work it. The louder the noise the more excited I became and then my cock exploded in my hand and onto the until then clean sheets. Sated, I reached to a box of tissues on the nightstand and wiped away my cum. As I did that, the noise in the other bedroom quieted and I pulled the blankets back over myself and I settled into a better sleep than I had been in before.

THE NEXT MORNING, I LAY QUIETLY IN THE SMALL BED and listened for sounds. Hearing none, I got up, and started to head for the hall bath. Then, thinking the better of going out bare chested lest it inspire mocking by our houseguest, I put my dress shirt on while still wearing my boxers and socks and ventured out of the room. Looking right, then left, I stepped out into the hall and into the bathroom. Once that was done, I went to the kitchen, filled the coffee maker, and began the process of caffeination. When the device had worked its magic, I strolled back to the bedroom to check my phone, which was on the nightstand. No messages, 12 emails, all junk. I ignored them, while I scrolled through the morning news until, finally, a text buzzed in from Diane.

2 Coffees . . . please

HMMPH, I thought. She expects me to bring her coffee. After what she did? Him too?

HMMPH, again. I was still indignant when I found myself in the kitchen filling two mugs and getting out the raw sugar and almond milk and adding it to her cup. As I was about to pick up the cups and grabbed my phone and messaged her back.

What In His?

Several seconds later, she responded.

3 Sugars

I pulled out the regular sugar and a teaspoon and I added it to Dan's coffee and picked up both cups and carried them to the bedroom door, and placing the cup beside the door, I knocked again.

"C'mon in. It's open," Dan said. So, turning the knob and pushing the door ajar, I reached down and retrieved the cup and entered the room only to encounter a jarring sight. Dan and my wife, laying naked holding each other on our uncovered bed. Diane's head rested comfortably on Dan's very hairy and heavily muscled chest, and his massive cock stood at full attention, like a flagpole, which I had no doubt she had saluted repeatedly the previous night and morning. As the night before, I worked very hard at not looking at the terrible, intimidatingly huge organ. Dan told me to put the cups on the nightstand and having done that I scurried away. I left without being acknowledged by my wife.

Going to the kitchen, I sat at the counter and tried to get my breath. Finally, it dawned on me my rush to be servile I'd not gotten coffee for myself. Walking over to the coffeemaker I pulled a cup off the rack and filled it, took a drink, and burned my lip. It was about that time that I heard the noise start again in my bedroom and as it became louder and more insistent. I felt my own loins stirring. Picking up my coffee I headed to the spare room, where I lay down on the small bed, slipped my boxer shorts off my hips, and began stroking my hardened cock to the rhythm of Diane's' moans and the thumping of the bed on the carpeted floor. Finally, I came, not hard by the standards set by Dan but hard by those I'd come to expect in my post pubescent life.

MUCH LATER, I LAY ON TOP OF THE COMFORTER on the small bed alone. I'd gone to refill my coffee twice and had jacked off three times and the sounds of passion from my bedroom had long since ceased, replaced by the sounds of the shower. One of them it seemed had decided to wash away the residue of the night and morning. Maybe both had. The thought excited me, and my overworked cock began once again to stir. Instead of reaching for my sore and reddened member, I reached for my coffee cup and found it to be empty. Swinging my legs off the bed, I stood with great effort and stretched. Looking down at my shirt front, there were stains from my morning's entertainment. I tried to wipe away the evidence with tissues and only caused a smear. So, I removed the shirt. Surely, they had gone back to bed again after showering. I decided to chance it. By the time I got back with fresh coffee, they'd be going at it again and I could listen to those horrible, terrible, arousing sounds.

I was standing at the counter in only my boxers and socks, waiting for the coffee maker to finish the brewing process when he came into the kitchen. Bare chested, carrying the shirt he wore the previous night. I was betting there were no semen stains on his shirt. Those were all on my bedsheets.

"Good morning, Jake," Dan said brightly. He got my name wrong again but looking at his impressive musculature I let it pass, and instead replied simply, "Morning."

We stood waiting for more coffee, and the gradual pace of the machine, made me want to shake it. I decided that would not hurry it along. It would only make a mess. I'd made enough messes so far today, and it wasn't noon yet. It didn't help that I felt puny alongside him. I wished he'd put on his shirt, or I could get mine, except if I did, he would see the evidence of my self-abuse. So, we stood. Just two guys waiting for coffee. Except one was much bigger than the other and one had spent the night fucking the other's wife. Other than that, just two guys. Waiting for coffee.

Then as if on cue, to ratchet up my tension another light year, Diane came into the kitchen. Thankfully, unlike Dan and myself, she was not shirtless. She meandered in sleepily wrapped in her fluffy white bathrobe. Her long blonde hair still looked damp, so that answered my question as to whether they showered together or alone. Well, I thought, at least we saved on the water bill. She first looked at Dan and stopping, leaned into him, and getting up on tiptoes, and kissed him on the lips. My traitorous cock twitched.

"Good morning, handsome," she said to him, and he grabbed her around the waist and pulled her to him.

"Good morning, again, beautiful," he replied. Finally, she looked at me with a small sheepish smile and said, "Morning honey." Instead of saying anything in reply, I looked away, saying instead.

"Coffee's ready."

BY THE TIME DAN WENT OUT THE DOOR, he had his shirt on, though not fully buttoned, giving the neighbors more fodder for gossip. He was carrying my best travel mug, with most of the second pot of coffee and about a pound of sugar. I secretly hoped he'd get diabetes. Diane walked him out and took a long time doing it. Ever the gentleman, he called to me from the entryway.

"Thanks, Jake." Then, I heard the door shut behind him and the big engine of his sportscar rev powerfully, and finally, Diane came slowly back into the kitchen, and we were finally alone.

"Here, if you need it so bad, let me help you," She began to stroke me slowly and carefully, and as the shame and guilt of my need began to build within me, I responded with a small but firm erection.

"So, was he . . . good?" I asked tentatively. She looked at me a bit as she stroked me, then a sly and knowing smile came across her face.

"So good," she told me, "So big. Well, you saw it. Huge. He's so good with it."

I felt my orgasm building and so did she.

"He made me cum so many times," she continued. "More in one night than you've made me cum in over three years." The statement made me wince, but my orgasm overcame my injured pride and she directed what ended in a few dribbles at my bare leg. Having done her duty, she let go and headed for the dressing area.

"You might want to get a Kleenex," she said as she walked away. "When you get cleaned you can make breakfast and we will plan our day."

"Mmmmm, the eggs are perfect, honey. Thank you." Diane ate with a hunger caused by strenuous sexual activity, as I pushed mine around my plate. Masturbation doesn't improve appetite whether it's done to you or self-inflicted.

By order of the carrier of our homeowner's insurance, Diane was not allowed to cook. In fact, she was allowed into the kitchen only for short, prescribed periods of time to do simple tasks such as getting coffee. She insisted the provision applied also to cleaning up. I was skeptical of that claim but didn't fight her on it. You know lawyers. Always reading the fine print.

"Once the dishes are done, let's change the sheets," she said. "Then, we can pick up the clothes. Where's your suit?" She must have finally noticed I wasn't in it, though I had taken off my cum-stained boxers and put on sleep pants and a Henley.

"In the spare room," I replied.

"Oh," was her response, as though in her frantic ardor she hadn't thought to consider where I had slept, or care.

"Well, then I suppose we need to change those sheets too," she said looking at me and grinning. I smiled back at her and nodded sheepishly. She laughed.

"Remember what your mama always said, Jackie, do it too much and you'll go blind," the comment made us laugh together.

"Can I just do it till I need glasses?" That caused us to giggle like two kids. The laughter soon settled down to smiles and as we looked at each other, and the fondness and indeed love we felt showed through, even after what had gone on the previous night.

"Thank you," she said with as much sincerity as any lawyer ever said anything. "Thank you for allowing me this freedom." Reaching out, we embraced. and I felt as close to her as her recent behavior had made me feel far away.

"After all," I said as I pressed my face to her luxurious hair." What's one night?"

Without missing a beat, or holding me any less tightly, my darling wife shattered any illusions I may have had.

"Oh, it's not one night honey," she said, as she squeezed me more fully to her considerable bosom. "Dan's coming back tonight." Releasing me from her embrace she started toward the bedroom, "In fact, we need to get moving. He'll be here before we know it and there's so much to do."

6

IANE FLEW INTO A FRENZY OF CLEANING and picking things up, the like of which I had never seen from her. All in preparation for the arrival of a man she hadn't known a full day. Had their acquaintance been a banana, it would be too green to eat. I tried in vain to keep up. Both with her white tornado cleaning regimen and in understanding her desire to impress "Dan the man." Failing at both I simply followed in her jet stream and did as I was told.

"Can you make some of those hot appetizers, I love, Jack? You know the ones I mean."

I did and told her I did. They were labor-intensive but were her favorite so, I assured her they would be hot and ready at the proper time.

"Oh goodie," she exclaimed happily. "Thank you, honey." She paused only slightly while dusting, which I watched in amazement. Not only that she was doing it, but that she knew how, and knew where to find the dust mop. As she flew around and made me do the same, I was reminded to call and cancel the cleaning lady for next week. Between that and saving on the water bill, having bulls over could be money-saving opportunities. However, my contemplation of the benefits of the situation was interrupted by a familiar bellow.

"Jack!" my wife said in her most commanding voice, "Get the sheets off the beds. Hurry, they need to be changed." She was in the bathroom scrubbing grout, and as I went by her toward our bedroom, she ducked her head out. "You may as well not change the sheets in the spare room. I have no doubt you'll just get them 'dirty' again." She said it teasingly. At least. I think she was teasing. Going into the bedroom, I pulled the comforter off our bed, then the sheets. The top sheet then the fitted sheet. As I picked up the pile, something fell out . . . They were Dan's briefs.

Pulling the linens back on the floor, I reached down and carefully pushed the shorts to look at them. They were big, and they were black made of that stretchy fabric that breathes, not mere cotton. I reached and picked them up carefully with the tips of my index finger and thumb. Looking at them I realized that the stretchiness was good because they were extremely "stretched out" in the crotch area. Having seen what, they were meant to contain I had great respect for the space-age material and wondered if I could buy stock. I picked up the whole mess and resolved to call my broker Monday.

Once I was done admiring my handiwork, I adjourned to the kitchen and began assembling the hors d'oeuvres. I decided to make three different kinds. The ones Diane loved ones I loved, and a third that we both liked. Variety is the spice of life. The oven was on and the ingredients (all of which we had, as luck would have it) out and at the ready. Puttering around the kitchen relaxed me and made me calmer than I'd been in days. Tonight, would be fun, in a normal, get to know each other way. Not in the bed breaking psychosexual way that had happened the night before. As the appetizers baked, their aroma started filling the kitchen.

"Something smells REALLY good," I heard Diane call from the other room. I wondered if she was still cleaning the bathroom. Surely not, even though cleaning was not her forte. Still, I hadn't seen her in a very long time, and looking at my watch I knew Dan's arrival was imminent. Opening the oven, I checked, and nothing was burned. In fact, they looked perfect. That being the case, I turned down the temp, to warm, closed the door, and went down the hall to find my wife. When I found her, she was sitting at her dressing table applying eye makeup. Expertly, I might add.

"You missed a spot," I kidded her. She hadn't heard me approach, but she didn't flinch. Diane was not given to being startled. Unlike me in the bar the night before.

She was wearing a pair of panties I did not recognize, not that I always got to see her underwear unless it was when it went in the wash. Funny, I thought, in my previous marriage I had done very few chores. A little cooking but Elizabeth did most everything. I didn't mind now. I liked taking care of Diane, even if I couldn't take care of her in all the ways she needed.

"Go to my closet and get me the red dress hanging on this end of the right side," She told me, and then added, "Please?"

I stepped inside the closet, which, as always looked like it had been organized by a hand grenade. One way in which I had no intention of taking care of Diane was by straightening out this mess. I took the red dress off the rack and held it in front of me. She had bought it two years and ten pounds before and had decided then it was "beyond the bounds of decency" to wear it in public. I carried it out and thought, "Oh well. If she wants to expose herself here at home to tease a guy she hardly knows, what's the harm?" She slipped the garment over her head and settled it onto her lush body, pulling and tugging and I realized, she wasn't going to put a bra on with it. I saw her nipples standing proud and prominent under the sheer fabric. Then I noticed the skirt was so short it came to the lower edge of her ass cheeks, and I knew staying home was the right thing to do. Once I could tear myself away from staring, I went to set up the bar.

The Scotch was ready. as was the vodka, which was Diane's drink of choice lately. Ice, glasses, cocktail napkins, limes, and lemons. If I wasn't the perfect husband, I was at least the perfect host. About the time, I was assessing my perfection, the front doorbell chimed. I started to go answer it. I was headed to the entryway when I heard Diane coming down the hall.

"I'll get it!! I'll get it!!!" She yelled and I wisely moved out of the way lest I be run over, and I was sure being stepped on by her would hurt. She was wearing a pair of shoes that perfectly matched her dress and had the highest heels I'd ever seen on her delicate feet. Regardless of that fact, she came down the hall and turned into the entry with the speed of a runaway train, and upon opening the door she squealed like she had sat bare assed on a block of ice.

"DAN," she cried out and he was barely through the door when she jumped into his arms.

The big man lifted her off the ground and spun her as easily as he might a feather. Then, placing her down before him, he held her and looked at her.

"There's my girl," he said and pulled her into a lengthy kiss.

She held him so close her nipples must have been drilling into the black suit coat and matching black shirt he wore over his masculine chest. What she said next rocked me, more than a little.

"How's the man of my dreams?" She said before they kissed again.

I didn't wait to hear the answer. I stepped back into the kitchen to check the hors d'oveures.

I left them alone for several minutes, to limit further humiliation. To stay busy. I took the trays out of the oven and placed their contents on plates to take to the bar. The little plates and utensils were already out. When I thought it was safe, I stepped to where I could be heard in the entry and called to Diane and Dan.

"Hey Dan," I said, "what can I get you to drink?" To which there was no response, so I went where I could see them. See them going out the door.

"Oh, honey," Diane said looking back, "Dan has reservations. He wanted to surprise me. We'll be back later tonight."

I didn't respond verbally but tried to smile tolerantly. Diane smiled back. Dan didn't smile back. He didn't look at me or acknowledge me. He had his hand on my wife's ass trying to grope her and hurry her to leave. He was obviously a talented multitasker.

The door closed behind them and I heard the car's big engine roar and its tires squeal as he rolled it out onto the street, leaving a smell of burning rubber behind as he attracted the attention of the neighborhood.

IT WAS MUCH LATER, AND I WAS STILL SITTING AT THE BAR. The hor d'oevres had gone uneaten and cold, but to make up for it, I had gotten very drunk very quickly and was now drinking some of the little bit of coffee left there from the morning. I was not getting more sober, but I was more awake. Being more awake had its drawbacks. It made me keenly aware of what had happened. My wife whom I adored had left with a younger, stronger more handsome man who was bigger and undoubtedly better than me in every way. She left and if I had stayed in the kitchen 30 seconds longer, she would have gone without so much as a goodbye. Of all the cuts I had received in the last 24 hours, that was the unkindest of all.

Or so I thought.

I was deep into my self-pity when a message beeped in from Diane. I saw her name come up and foolish hope rose and filled my chest. Dan had been an ass, and I needed to get her. I better have more coffee. Then I read the message.

When we come back, you'll be in the spare room, right?

I took the scotch bottle and poured some in my coffee cup and felt my resolve strengthen to iron. I'd ignore her message. I'd make her guess. Furthermore, when they returned. I'd be asleep in my own bed, and they could go to hell.

Then, the reality of the situation hit, as it had the previous night, and the thing that turned to iron was my treacherous cock, and because of that, I did return her message.

Yes!

7

DIANE AND DAN CAME STUMBLING IN around 2:30 a.m. and not quietly. By then, they were drunk, and I was sober, and awake before I heard the clatter they created trying to get to my bedroom (not the one I was occupying, but the one I was paying for). Around 12:30, I quit the coffee and went back to scotch, and by the time I lie down in the spare bedroom the two were battling in my system. The scotch finally won, and I dropped off to fitful sleep where I had nightmarish dreams of my wife being kidnapped by a monster in a two-piece suit, who sucked her nipples till she squirted milk like the fountains in Seville, Spain. Then once I was awake, the coffee won the final battle. So, the loud thump they made when he must have slammed my wife's body up against the wall, didn't roust me so much as arouse me, and my groin tingled, and that area of my body was awake too and the sheet covering me began to tent. Granted, it was a pup tent, but still, a tent is a tent.

Once I heard them in the other bedroom (my bedroom), I reached under the sheets and pulled my cock out of my sleep pants and began a steady rhythm of stroking. As my erection (small as it was), built, my movements were in time with the sounds of furious fucking taking place in the next room. The thumping. My wife's moaning. Until, finally, I couldn't hold back any longer, and I came. Hard. Spurting what by my standards was a large amount of semen on the sheets I hadn't changed. Afterward, I lay spent. Totally limp, and not just my cock. My body seemed boneless, weightless, and vaguely tingling. When my nerve endings finally calmed down, I began to doze. As I was drifting off, I realized the noises next door had stopped and that room was quiet too. That's the point at which I finally went into a restful sleep, with no dreams of monsters, whether dressed in suits or not.

WHEN I AWOKE, SUNSHINE WAS FILTERING in through the blinds. Then I heard a door opening and felt someone's weight on the bed beside me, accompanied by the smell of coffee.

"Good morning, Sleepyhead." It was Diane's voice, speaking to me softly, in soothing tones. She touched me gently, and I rolled onto my back and looked up. The light hitting just the edge of her face looked like a halo and made her look like an angel. She could be angelic, but her halo was often held up by a set of horns. The last few days the horns seemed to be overwhelming the halo. Here she was, with me again, her sunlit face smiling sweetly, bringing me a cup of coffee.

Coffee?

"Hi sweetheart," I said and looked at what she was offering as "coffee," suspiciously. Don't get me wrong. I appreciated the gesture. She still cared enough to show consideration and indeed, tenderness. The Diane I knew, had no concept of any kitchen appliance, including the coffeemaker. If she had to boil water, she would have to Google the recipe. So, I regarded the beverage with a jaded eye. Taking the cup, I could feel it was hot. That's a start, I thought. I sniffed it. Smells right, I thought. Knowing my wife as I did, God only knows what was in there. The question I had to ask myself, "are you brave enough to drink it?" Looking up, Diane was watching with such expectancy. So beautiful, her ripe body barely contained in the fluffy white bathrobe that I had washed the previous day. Looking at it I briefly considered the possibility it would need washing again.

Gingerly, I took a sip. Tasted right. Another longer sip. It wasn't killing me.

"This is good Diane," I said. "Very good." I sipped a little more and my curiosity overcame my gratitude." I hate to say this, I never knew you could work the coffeemaker." She giggled softly.

"Well," she admitted," There was a YouTube video explaining this model. I followed that."

I sipped more coffee, considered what she had done for me, and felt, glad and grateful to have such a thoughtful wife.

"Aww, thank you, sweetie. It was so nice of you to go to such trouble so you could bring me coffee," I told her.

She smiled.

"Well, Dan, got me up early, and after . . . well you know . . . he wanted coffee." That explained a lot. As she spoke, she reached and pulled the robe around her a little more fully, out of some attempt at modesty. Watching her make the move, all I could think was "It's a little late for that, isn't it?" I thought it but didn't say it as she continued speaking.

"I was going to wake you up to make it, but you were sleeping so soundly, I didn't have the heart. So, I decided I'd try myself," she said proudly. All I could think was the sleep I had been in must have been a deep one. Or the morning's sexual escapades were much quieter than they had been having. Blow jobs are quiet. The thought made my cock twitch, but my wife couldn't see it under the sheet. A good thing, though I was beginning to wonder if I now enjoyed my coffee with a side of humiliation.

"Anyway, we were so trashed last night we took an Uber and left his car," She explained as I sipped what I was an excellent cup of coffee. "So, it's still at the bar. I told Dan you'd be happy to get up and take us to get it," She leaned forward so her breasts fell out of her half open robe, dangling enticingly before my open mouth. I was sure it was not an accident. Pretty sure, at least. Whatever it was, distracted me enough and I agreed to get his car. She headed to the door without closing the robe, as she said, "Okay, but we need to get moving. Dan's got tickets to today's game, so I need to be ready." Then having made her exit, she poked her head in the door.

"You'll make us breakfast, won't you? Nothing too hard. French toast. That's Dan's favorite."

8

THE DISHES WERE LEFT IN THE SINK so I could load Dan and Diane into the car so he could get his car and they could make it to the stadium in time for the kickoff. Diane looked great (as usual) with all the team swag I had bought her in our time together. As they exited my SUV Dan thanked me and called me Jake again. Diane gave me a sisterly peck on the cheek while looking nervously to make sure he didn't see. Once he had her in the car he grabbed her, pulled her across the console, and gave her a long, passionate kiss which he made certain I DID see. They then sped off, again, 20 MPH too fast, so they could sit in pregame traffic jams for the next two hours. I, on the other hand, turned toward home, (at 5 MPH under the posted speed limit), where I would load the dishwasher, change the sheets (both beds this time), and watch the game alone.

Football Sundays had always been our time, and in fact for many years, even before we were "us" I had season tickets. Diane hated going when it was rainy, snowy, cold, or windy. (It messed up her hair), or most anytime it wasn't sunny and 70. So, I dropped the tickets, and we would watch with friends at different local bars, or at home, just us. She had explained as she supervised me making

Dans French Toast, Dan was a season ticket holder, so football was now, "their" thing," at least for that week. The team had a Monday night game the next week. We were scheduled to watch it with friends. I was hoping things would blow over by then. We were hosting a BBQ at the house, so at least I'd have her for that Sunday. Meanwhile, I was on my third beer and the game was out of hand in our favor, when I decided to go sit in the backyard. The leaves had begun turning and the seasonal flowers were almost gone. The grass had been recently mowed and there was still a faint smell of its irrigated sweetness.

I sat on the glider. It had been bought for Diane, for us to sit in together. Watch the grandkids play as we grew old together (when grandkids were provided by my three kids, that is). The last few days proved to me how much closer I was to being old than my wife. I still felt young. Vigorous in most ways. Since Friday, the facts had come home (literally) and smacked me in the face. Keeping up with a man 15 years younger, seven inches taller, six inches "longer." was a fool's errand. I sat there for a very long time until finally, I heard sounds in the entryway. Getting up off the glider, I went back in the house and heard voices. Dan and Diane. We got to the kitchen simultaneously. My wife was holding a big foam finger and a stack of commemorative beer cups. Dan was holding my wife. He saw me and spoke first.

"Hey, Jake," he said it in a way I knew was no innocent mistake, which was annoying. The really, hurtful part was that Diane didn't correct him. She merely smiled at him as if he had made a joke and put the cups in the sink and the foam finger on the counter, while Dan went to the fridge and helped himself to one of my beers.

"Dan wanted to leave early to avoid traffic," Diane explained while "the man of her dreams" popped the top off the bottle, leaving the cap on the counter for me to throw away.

"She wanted to leave at halftime," Dan explained taking a big drink. "but, I explained to her, we'd get arrested 'doing it' in the parking lot. So, she parked her hot little ass in the seat, and she finally got me outta there midway through the third quarter."

Still holding the bottle, he curled his free arm around Diane's waist and reached down the front of her jeans, which was amazing considering how tight she wore them.

"We didn't get arrested, did we, baby?" She said and snickered as he bit the nape of her neck. The bite and the memory made her blush, but also giggle both made me cringe.

"I need the bathroom, baby," He looked around, then I realized the only one he'd ever used was the one in our bedroom. I pointed to the hall.

"First door on the left," I said, feeling lucky my wife didn't go with him as he pissed. Once he was gone, Diane leaned on the counter, as I went to the fridge to get one of my beers before they were all gone.

"Get me one too, will you, honey." She asked and I pulled out two, twisted the top off one, and handed her the bottle. I opened the other, putting the cap next to Dan's. Then looking at them, I picked up all three, carried them to the trash, and came back to my beer.

"Hey, honey," She said almost sweetly, "what do we have in the fridge for dinner?"

Naming off several things I could turn into an edible meal she smiled as sweetly as she had spoken.

"I was bragging on you yesterday, to Dan." I already knew where this was going, but I was patient enough to wait and see how she got there.

"You don't suppose you could be persuaded to make us dinner?" At the end of her plea, she was almost cooing. She looked at me and I swore she batted her eyes, then she took a sip of beer, taking the bottle's neck between her lips in a very seductive fashion.

"Please?" This time she batted her eyes. I was sure of it. "I'll make sure you get a special treat later." The beer bottle got another blowjob, but it was gratuitous. I was hooked. About that time, Dan came back from the bathroom.

"Jack's making us dinner, darling." She told Dan before he grabbed her, spun her around, and bent her backward with a volcanic kiss that reflected the longing that came from not having seen each other for almost five minutes. Once the kiss broke off, he released her and she staggered slightly and gasped for breath, holding the edge of the countertop to stay upright. Watching the spectacle, made my cock twitch. Before it had time to fully engorge, Dan clapped his hands and rubbed them together in what I sensed was an expression of impatience more than enthusiasm.

"Awright," he exclaimed. "So, what's for dinner and when do we eat?"

9

As it turns out, the answers were: Chicken piccata after they'd had three drinks, made and served by me. Diane was once again having vodka straight up with a twist, and I cut myself cutting the twist of lemon. Which is not to say she didn't pitch in. She took on the arduous task of entertaining our guest in the living room. Staying out of the kitchen was always my wife's best contribution to meal preparation.

"Very good, Jake," Dan said as I delivered their first round of drinks. "Diane, he does this very well. There is a career in service for this boy." My wife laughed again without comment, as her lover continued." We really need to get him to dress the part next time. Black slacks, white shirt. Maybe a nice tie and a bar towel draped over his arm." I pretended to be laughing and Diane really was when she finally said to him, "Stop." but not like she meant it, since it ended in her laughing so much that she spilled some vodka on the coffee table.

"See, Jake? A bar towel on the arm would have come in really handy now." She snickered as he said it. I fetched a kitchen towel and wiped up the spill, after which I stood and saw Dan looking at me. I knew he was going to say something, and that it would be something I wouldn't like.

"I know what he needs," the big man said with great fake conviction. "Not for serving drinks, but when he's cooking, to protect the white shirt, an apron."

"Well," I countered, "I do have an apron."

"Yes, he does," Diane told him, "It says, 'kiss the cook.'"

Dan's smile broadened, and my stomach tightened. He was about to say something deeply insulting. I had only known him for two days, but I was sure of it.

"Well, frankly I'd rather not," he said. "Though if he was to insist . . ." The sentence trailed off for comedic effect as he watched my discomfort. So did my wife who said nothing, and only laughed. What they did not see was my arousal. My cock was stiffening more with each insult and slight. Then he continued the barrage.

"No, your husband needs a nice frilly apron. Pink, with ruffles," he declared, and though he laughed, Diane was positively doubled over. Smiling tolerantly, I exited to the kitchen, with Jake calling after me to let them know when dinner was ready.

Dinner was ready after two more drinks each. Both times I draped a white bar towel over my forearm, letting my loving wife collapse into paroxysms of laughter again at her boyfriend's abuse of me. She did not, but I was ready just in case. In any event, he was too busy groping Diane to be very abusive toward me. Then, finally, all the courses were ready, and the lovers were called to the dining room. Ever the gentleman, Dan held Diane's chair for her, and she sat looking up at him so admiringly, no one would ever guess I'd done that every time we had eaten together for three and a half years. Then going to the chair directly to her left, he stood beside it and waited. I looked at him, and, waited. Then looked again, and realized, he expected me to pull out his chair. My blood pressure, though normally high, must have gone through the roof. Anger welled within and froze me, as Dan and Diane both looked at me expectantly. Then I felt my cock swelling, again and it prompted me to action, as I meekly stepped to the dining table and pulled the big man's chair out for him, and he sat, not looking at me, but at Diane. On his face was a broad smile of triumph.

Next, I decanted the wine and was about to pour it when Dan cleared his throat.

"Mind if I see the cork?" He asked as though it was a request, though I knew it was an expectation. Placing the wine bottle back on the sideboard, I retrieved the cork and taking it to the table, handed it to Dan. He sniffed contemplatively and handed it back as Diane watched each move he made with admiration. She might have been unfamiliar with the process because I had never done it, because cork sniffing was pretentious bullshit. Once I had put the well-sniffed cork on the sideboard, I brought back the wine. It was a California Pinot Grigio of good vintage and one of Diane's favorites. As I was about to pour her some wine, Dan cleared his throat again and held up his glass.

"I'd like to taste it first," He stated it flatly. No feigned request this time. I looked at my wife and she was smiling in obvious delight. Moving the wine bottle to his glass, he held his hand out with his fingers an inch apart.

"Just a taste," he emphasized. "That much. You know, about the length of your dick."

Diane put her hands over her mouth and burst out laughing. I felt the color rise in my face, as I blushed in shame. I also felt blood rushing to another body part and realized I was very aroused and excited. I carefully placed the neck of the bottle to the rim of his glass and poured in about half an inch of the wine. He looked at the glass, then at me, and picking up the glass he took the half-inch of wine into his mouth and held it, then swished it, then swallowed it.

"That will be fine," he said without looking at me. "You may pour for the lady and me." Which I did, and when I went to fill my own glass, I saw my place setting, which had been immediately to Diane's right, as close to her as his, on the near end of the table, was now at the far end. I saw I had been moved so I'd be eating in another zip code from them. I looked at my wife and she wouldn't raise her eye from her wine glass. Dan on the other hand was looking at me intently, gauging my attitude. His mouth was a smug smile, and he nodded slightly toward Diane, who spoke.

"We . . . we thought we needed some . . . room," she stammered.

I looked at my wife questioningly, then at her lover, then down the table to the place that had been set for me.

"You may serve," Dan told me, in a steady authoritative voice. "Salad first, then the entrees."

So, I did, placing their salads first then mine, as well as pouring myself some wine, which I desperately needed. My salad was only half gone when Dan signaled, they were ready for their entrees. He did it by tapping his water glass with his teaspoon. When I looked up, he made an open palm gesture toward his and Diane's salad plates.

"You may serve the entrees," I was told, and for some reason that only my tingling groin could explain, I abandoned my half-eaten salad to comply. In fact, I jumped out of my chair and went quickly to the kitchen and took the piccata out of the warmer and put it on plates, topping it with the caper sauce and lemon slices. Finally, steamed asparagus spears were added and I carried two of the plates to the dining room, only to be met by Dan's withering gaze. It stopped me for a beat and then, I proceeded to carefully set the plates in front of first Diane and then started to place Dans and he cleared his throat. I realized I was approaching from his right. Moving around to his other side, I corrected the potential faux pas.

Stopping, I looked to see he was smiling at my wife, and, saying, as though I wasn't there. "See, darling, you were wrong. He is trainable." With that comment still ringing in my ears, I slunk off to retrieve my own dinner.

The rest of the dinner went off with minimal embarrassment on my part since I remembered how waiters acted and reacted in the many finer restaurants I had patronized throughout my life. Being from a monied family had deprived me of the experience of working in such an environment, but my wife and her lover were going to help me make up for lost time.

I was still cleaning the stove, the oven, and what seemed like every dish and glass in the house, even as I made and carried an endless stream of drinks to Diane and Dan who were sitting together in the living room watching Amazon Prime. Or should I say glancing at it in between kissing and groping each other? Had I wanted to insert a piece of tissue paper between them, it would not have been possible, and I was mystified how the drinks disappeared so quickly since they did not seem to break from their passionate embrace even when I brought in refills. The next day was Monday, and Diane had promised me a "special treat earlier in the day. So, it was with great optimism when finally, I wiped clean the last smear and put away the last dish, went into the living room, and saw them both getting off my couch. She could escort him to the door, kiss him goodnight, and my wife and I would once more be alone.

It was a nice dream, but in my dreams, Dan didn't flip me his car keys.

"Be a sport," he said, "and get my bag, will you Jake?"

As he walked toward my bedroom, with his arm around my wife, he added: "There's a garment bag in the trunk. Oh, and my shaving kit. You can bring them to me in here, and don't forget to lock it."

As I hauled Dan's luggage out of his car and into my house, I wasn't sure what shocked me more. That he was staying another night, or that he had a shaving kit. The three-day growth of beard seemed ubiquitous. How did a guy maintain that and shave too? The mystery of Dan's whiskers was however replaced in my mind by a deep disappointment. My "special treat" would obviously be put on hold or canceled, and as I opened the door to our bedroom, I determined I would put on a brave face. It was like in baseball. Guys who get hit by a pitch can't let the pain show. So, I rubbed a little dirt on it and hung Dan's garment bag in Diane's closet and turned as if I was expecting a quarter as a tip. What I got was a correction. This time from my wife.

"Can you please put that in the other closet, Jack?" She said impatiently. "You know, I don't have a spare inch of room in mine."

Properly chastened, I went sheepishly to the closet (her closet) and got the garment bag and carried it to the "other" closet (my closet) and placed Dan's shaving kit beside the sink in the bathroom. Then I returned to them expecting either goodnight or get out or both, depending on the urgency of their horny needs. Getting neither, I tried to mitigate the awkward pause by stepping toward the door to make a strategic exit from what was normally my bedroom with my wife, but the last few days had become a den of iniquity. However, Dan took two steps to the side and easily used his big body to block my escape.

"Whoa, there, pal," he said as I stopped. "Your wife told me she made you a promise earlier tonight. If you made dinner. Which you did."

Confused, but fearful, I looked at Diane, who would not look back, peering instead into the open door into her closet. Perhaps wondering how she could make more space. I on the other hand was wondering how I could get the floor to open and swallow me whole. I turned my gaze back to Dan, hoping her wondering produced a better result than mine.

"The dinner was . . . fine, by the way," he began condescendingly.: "So since you followed through, I felt . . . we felt," He said it as he pulled my wife to him, "You should get your little treat."

Having said that, Dan looked at Diane, then Diane looked at Dan then both looked at me, and he elbowed her gently, which made her giggle nervously.

"Drop your pants," she told me. The words shocked me, and I stood without moving, unsure if I could even breathe as Dan smirked watching my unease. I shook my head slightly, and Dan elbowed her again.

"C'mon," she said impatiently, "Do you want your treat or not? Drop em. Let's get this over with."

They stood glaring at me waiting.

"Jack, you know you want it. Just drop your pants and let me do it to you. Or would you rather just go into the other room and beat it silly like you've been doing?"

"No," Dan asserted, "He wants it and I want to see it." He released my wife, straightened to his full height, and flexed slightly, to appear menacing. It worked and I unbuckled my belt. He was watching me very closely as I unbuttoned my jeans and let them fall lower on my hips. His reaction was to make a gesture that indicated to me he wanted them lower, so I pushed until they were around my ankles.

"Now drop your shorts," Diane ordered. "Or do I have to do it for you?" My head shook again, and I hooked my thumbs in the waistband of my cotton boxers and started to lower them.

"To be honest," the big man said to my wife, "I expected panties, to which she slapped his arms playfully and laughed. Once the smooth fabric was below my groin, he was the one laughing.

"OH WOW," Dan exclaimed. "When you told me he was small, I had NO idea." Then he crouched down theatrically and got very close to get a better look.

"You poor girl," he said to Diane. "No wonder you were so starved."

Satisfied he had humiliated me sufficiently, for the time being, he stood and stepped out of Diane's way.

"Okay," he told her. "Go to it."

That's all the encouragement my wife needed to grab my stiffened member and "get it over with." She began stroking slowly, but quickly picked up speed and as she stroked, Dan stepped to the bathroom and got a towel, spreading it in front of me.

"Don't want you lovebirds making a mess," He explained, and it was just in time, as my orgasm overcame me and spilled semen onto the towel saving the carpet from stains. Dan clapped at my climax, and I blushed, as Diane quickly released her grip and stepped back next to her lover and away from me.

"Well, dear," Dan said to her, "Not one of your better organ recitals. It has to be tough when you have to play the piccolo. "She smiled at his mocking reference to me and replied. "Well, now I'm ready for the whole brass band," Then looking at me as though I was a bug, she said, "You're dismissed."

Then once I was in the spare room my phone dinged. It was a text from Diane.

Coffee at 6:30.

10

GETTING UP TO GET THEM COFFEE AT 6:30 was no problem since I virtually never slept. I collapsed on the small bed emotionally and mentally exhausted and sexually sated, but with their laughter still ringing in my ears. It caused my sleep to be fragmented and nightmare filled, broken up only by the frequent periods of masturbation. Getting out of bed was a temporary relief for my red and overly abused dick. First, there was coffee, then I made them breakfast, and then they were out the door. Dan before Diane, but not enough time in between departures to ask the inevitable question "will you be seeing him again?" One quick, perfunctory peck on the cheek and she was in the garage, pulling her car out and heading for the office. Leaving me alone. Like I was and had been most days since I took a "golden parachute" from the insurance company where I'd been an executive. That was over two years before and I did it thinking Diane and I would have more time together. We traveled some at first, but Diane's legal work always seemed to get in the way. I told her that she didn't still need to practice, and she seemed insulted and said I was minimizing her work. Finally, I resigned myself to the fact I'd have to travel alone or be at home waiting for her to return from the office. Which I did, and gradually became a "house husband." The last few days had left me even more time alone to think. I had concluded that as much as my sexual shortcomings, my house husband status had diminished me in my wife's eyes. Feeling that from her had only made my ED worse and eventually led us to the past weekend. Which until that point I had considered an isolated "sowing of wild oats." As I sat drinking the dregs of the cold coffee they had left, I wondered if this was now a "new reality." Was this an anomaly, or was it now my life?

5:30 Diane's usual arrival time came and went and no Diane. Finally, I got a text.

Bringing home takeout. Thai, ok?

I messaged back Thai was fine, not only because I liked Thai food, but also because she could have brought me horse shit to eat, I would have been happy because that meant she was coming home. When she arrived (alone) I was overjoyed. Giddy as a kid on Christmas morning. It would be just us again. I didn't ask. I was afraid to ask and as Monday flowed into Tuesday, Wednesday and Thursday I became more and more optimistic. Oh, on some level I was disappointed. It had been a wild and exciting weekend. Arousing, even for me, and especially for her. It was not real life, and the consequences could be disastrous. Both for our relationship and her career. As she once again kissed my cheek before leaving Friday morning, I was confident Dan was merely a fond memory on her part. Sometime far in the future, she could look for another, less controlling man. Hopefully, one who was not so mean to her loving husband.

After she kissed me, she stopped. The way she looked at me shriveled my confidence in direct proportion to the shriveling of my cock.

"Can you be a dear and clean the house today? Change the sheets and all? Dan's staying the weekend."

After lobbing that grenade, she spun on her high heels and headed to her car. The garage door went up the engine revved, and she was gone. I stood still stunned. When I finally recovered my senses, I had so many thoughts, but one stood out.

At least she didn't call me Jake.

11

Time crawled at the start and accelerated commensu-rate with the knot I got in my stomach which corresponded directly with the solidity of my erection. My entire body conflicted with itself until Diane arrived at 4:00, 90 minutes early. She was armed with several shopping bags from major department stores. Major and pricey, and there were enough she needed me to go to the garage and bring in a second load. She hung much of it in the closet. The same closet where she had so little room the previous weekend. The rest went into her lingerie drawers and on her shoe racks. She was shuffling things around when she called me over and handed me a list.

"Here," she told me, "Go to the store and get all this, and hurry. Dan will be here at 7."

Beating a hasty retreat, I looked at the list and planned my route. Much of it was liquor and beers of different types. Two things were apparent. While we shared a taste for the same woman, our taste in ales and lagers was different. Secondly, he had become bored with only drinking all my Johnny Blue. The rest of the list was food-stuffs, mostly very high grade. I'd have to go to a specialty store to get those. On my way back, I made a quick detour to the drug store, to get condoms and though I didn't know his exact size, I could guess and so I bought "Extra-large." They came in 12 packs. I bought two and hoped that would be enough for their weekend of bliss. I finally got back home at 5:30.

"Diane?" I called down the hall as I brought the package in from the garage. "Honey, I'm home." She didn't respond, so after putting the beer and refrigerated food in the fridge, the booze behind the bar, and the rest in the pantry, I took the two boxes of extra-large protection and went toward the back of the house to give them to my wife. There were sounds coming from our bedroom, so that's where I went, and what I saw jolted me. Piles of my clothing on the bed. Then my wife almost knocked me down rushing out of my closet carrying several of my suits and shirts on hangers. She took them out of the bedroom.

"Grab the shit on the bed and bring it in here, okay?" She said as she hurried past. She had taken a left. I could guess her destination. Stunned and empty-handed I headed into the spare bedroom where my wife was throwing my clothes on the room's small bed. She saw me enter and gave me a look I interpreted as disapproval.

"Hurry," She exclaimed, "he'll be here before we know it."

"What are you doing?" I asked in disbelief at what was obviously happening. My wife was moving me out of our bedroom. Diane stopped and stared at me blankly, then my words finally seemed to register. and a thin smile crossed her lovely face.

"This is just to give Dan some room. He's bringing clothes over," she explained. As she told me, she noticed my crestfallen look, and came over to me and put her arms around me tenderly, not like a wife comforting her husband. Like an adult placating a petulant child.

"Help me out on this, please?" She said it as an "ask," but I knew it was not. This was an expectation. Deep down, I knew it was time to stand up, to push back. All I can say now is, I desperately hoped, no prayed that this was as far as it went. That if I accepted this indignity at her hands that would be enough. She'd be satisfied and it would all blow over. One last wild weekend and life as we knew it would resume. So, I caved.

"How much do you want to move?" I asked meekly as she pushed her ample bosom to my thin chest. Then, she lifted her face and looked at me with a smile that was angelic but contained a hint of Lucretia Borgia. The smile and loved and to which I could never say no.

"Oh, not much," she replied. "Here lets, go and I'll show you."

Not much turned out to be most of it, along with my toiletries going into the guest bath. Once the change had been finished, I saw the bag from the drugstore laying where I'd dropped it in shock. Picking it up, I handed it to my wife, who had begun undressing so she could shower.

"Here, sweetheart," I said sheepishly. "I bought these for you. Well for Dan really. In case you ran out of the last box."

She took the bag and looked in and her expression caused me to expect her to say something like "How quaint." But she thanked me for being thoughtful and removing the boxes from the bag put them on the nightstand and she continued taking off her clothes as I watched. She was going through the piece-by-piece process of removal and as she did, throwing each item on the floor, knowing I would pick them up once she was in the shower.

Finally, her firm breasts standing out proud, strong, and completely bare, she slid off her panties. Then I saw an unfamiliar sight. Her pubic hair once neatly trimmed was now gone. Her mound smooth as an egg. I stared in disbelief, and she noticed my stare.

"Cool huh?" She said happily and then ran her fingers across her pussy and purred. "So smooth."

"How . . . when . . .?" I sputtered. She laughed at my confusion.

"I had it waxed Monday after work," That explained why she said she was "still too sore" to even discuss sex all week. It wasn't from Dans huge cock. It was from the depilation. Taking my hand, she placed it on her mound moving my fingers carefully with her own.

"See?" She told me. "Feel how smooth it is?"

Nodding weakly, my fingers began to roam, as though taking on a mind of their own. They received a hard slap for their trouble. Not the playful slaps like she had given her lover. This was a punitive rap across the knuckles about the time I had begun to probe her pussy lips.

"Stop," she demanded, "I need to get ready," "Having said that, she went to the shower, and I stood a while letting it all sink in. Finally, I roused myself into action and began picking up my wife's discarded clothes and separating the items to be laundered from those needing dry cleaning. Finally, I retrieved her panties from where she had discarded them. Lifting the delicate lace garment to my face, I inhaled her scent and was transported back in time, to days and nights when she used to lie to me that "size doesn't matter" and sex was a frequent feature of our relationship.

"Like that huh?" Diane's voice startled me, and I jumped slightly and dropped the panties. She sauntered past me, her luscious body still slightly damp. She bent and picked up her underwear and held them close to my nose.

"Here, get a good whiff," she said mockingly as she then dropped them on the bed and dried herself. As she did, she laughed.

Once she had dried herself sufficiently, she looked at her panties, then she looked at me, then back at the panties and there was that smile again. The Lucretia Borgia smile. Seeing it scared me, but my cock twitched in response.

"Hmmm," she muttered contemplatively, "You really like my panties, don't you?" I nodded wordlessly as she continued.

"Since I won't be wearing any panties tonight, maybe you should."

Just when I thought my wife's behavior couldn't shock me more than it already had, it did. She picked up the pink lacy undergarment and held them to me.

"Here, honey," she said teasingly. "Put them on."

Taking them from her, I looked at them and my cock twitched and stiffened. She smiled at me encouragingly.

"It will make me so hot if you do it," she told me. "If you do, I'll give you another special treat."

I looked at her skeptically. It was a look meant to indicate that getting me to do something so perverse would require more than the promise of a hand job. She understood my hesitancy and upped the stakes.

"If you wear them tonight," she offered, "I'll let you lick my pussy." Reaching down she rubbed her palm over it and purred.

"My smooth, sexy pussy." She licked her lips as she did it and I was enthralled. "Think of it Jackie, no flossing."

As I watched I realized it was a performance, designed to seduce me to do as she wanted. I didn't bother to wonder how many times in three and a half years she'd done it or how many times it had succeeded. Most would have been the answer, but I didn't ask. I simply agreed.

"Okay," I said grudgingly, "I'll wear them."

My words made her positively giddy, and she giggled and clapped her hands, as I slowly undid my belt, kicked off my shoes, and lowered my pants, stepping out, leaving me in only my underwear. I held the panties and looked, unsure they'd fit, but afraid, they would. Laying them aside, I slid my boxers down and stepped out of them and stood naked before her.

"Ooooh," she cooed, "the lil guy seems as excited as I am. How nice, I love it." Then she giggled again, and she watched anxiously as I slid into the slinky panties, and I heard her suck in a big breath. I pulled them till they sat low on my hips and when they were there, they would go no farther.

"Take away your hands, so I can see," Seeing led to further cooing which led to more gleeful clapping.

"Turn around," she directed me to pirouette as she watched attentively and finally told me to put my pants back on.

"Oh, pick up your man's underwear and put them in the hamper," she ordered. "You won't be needing those anymore."

12

"**J**UST WAIT TILL YOU SEE," Diane was laughing so hard she could barely speak, and she escorted the newly arrived, Dan, down the hall to the bedroom, where I had taken his suitcases and garment bags. I had brought them in myself, as he had been too fully occupied molesting my wife in the living room after I had brought him a drink. Now, with molestation finished for the moment, and his drink empty and with no one to make a new one, they came back for what I feared would be another humiliation for yours truly. When they appeared in the open door, both were still laughing. Ironically enough, I was unpacking the case containing his briefs a fact not lost on Dan.

"I shoulda known," Dan said while holding my wife tightly around her slender waist. "That I'd find him fondling my underwear." As always, Diane laughed, as I put the stretchy garments in my now empty drawers.

"Do you wanna see?" She asked him, eager for my further debasement.

"Of course, I want to see," He said agreeably, "Although I've got to say, I'm a little jealous of how much more anxious you are for your husband to drop his pants before you get me to drop mine." Diane frowned and shook her head at him. Then she leaned her face up to his and they kissed, passionately as I watched.

"It's for a different reason silly," as she frowned and shook her head at him. Then, turning to me she smiled broadly and said, "Let's see." All I could think as I undid my belt and unbuttoned my jeans is that if she'd had this much enthusiasm for having me drop my pants before this, we wouldn't have needed to find a bull. But she didn't and we did, and so it was with that reality in mind that I lowered my pants and gave my wife and her boyfriend another reason to laugh at me.

Dan's laughter as I stood there in Diane's panties had to violate local noise ordinances. Then, to make matters worse, he had me do a pirouette like Diane had, which was harder in that my jeans were around my ankles.

"They look a little loose in the crotch," he joked as he reached and pulled at the fabric at the front of the garment. Diane snickered as I blushed again at her boyfriend's mocking.

"Those look good on him," he said as he took Diane in his arms as I watched.

"Maybe from now on, we should call him Jacklyn."

Then, he turned toward the door, he headed out into the hall with my wife beside him.

"Okay, shows over," he decreed as he walked toward the living room. Pull up your pants and let's go in here. I need another drink and then Diane and I have reservations for dinner."

Both had one drink and kissed hungrily between sips, and then they were out the door, and I was left alone, which was best. As much as Dan had wanted a drink after my "little show," I desperately needed one.

THEY GOT BACK EARLY THE NEXT MORNING. He must have slowed down his drinking because he drove. They came in noisily and their lovemaking after they got in the bedroom was no quieter than their entrance. Diane was moaning and screaming, and both were calling to their creators. It went on a long time and then there was quiet. Till my phone beeped in a text message:

Come join us if you want your treat

I read it twice wondered if I was about to receive more "manual labor" courtesy of my beautiful life. If not, then a treat is truly what this would be, for her too. While my cock was small and undependable, my tongue was skilled and strong and I flew out of bed, overjoyed that after a long hiatus I was once again going to be allowed to give her pleasure. I was also feeling smart at having gotten the new boxes of condoms. Pregnancy and STD's notwithstanding, tasting latex and spermicidal lubricant was better than the alternative. I was wearing a t-shirt and hastily pulling my sleep pants on my naked bottom half when another text buzzed in:

Be sure you are wearing the panties

SO SEXY XXX

I had removed and placed Diane's used underwear on my pillow when I began my almost nonstop masturbation marathon, which only stopped when sleep overcame me. I was awake now and found them beside where I had laid my head. Pulling them back on I headed to my real bedroom, so I didn't miss my chance. I left on my T-shirt so I wouldn't be cold and was immediately rebuked upon entering the presence of my wife and her lover.

"What's that?" She asked testily. "A t-shirt? That's been the problem," she said to Dan. "He has this weird version of sexy." I stood as she shook her head sadly and renewed her verbal assault. "It's not sexy. Take off the fucking t-shirt." Which I did, exposing my thin almost hairless chest, and slight belly. Dan and Diane meanwhile were laying on the bed, with the top sheet covering their lowers areas, the rest of their perfect bodies mocking me.

I stood in Diane's lacy pink panties, trying not to tremble in excitement. She and Dan both smiled at me in ways that made my attempt to not tremble impossible. It was a combination of excitement mixed with humiliation and fear. Diane crooked her index finger urging me to come toward her. Which I did. When I got to the edge of the bed Dan pulled the sheet off my wife and she spread her legs.

"Come," she said. "You can lick me just like I promised. This is how you can make me feel good."

She patted the spot between her legs, and I crawled up onto the bed. As I got closer, I saw how her pussy lips glistened in the bedroom ambient light. I took it as a signal of her arousal and eagerly buried my face in her sopping wet mound. Delving deeper, I tasted something strange. Something different. It wasn't latex. It wasn't lube. It was the taste of what had to be Dans cum. I lifted my head and looked at the nightstand, at the boxes of condoms I had bought, both were unopened. I tried to pull away in shock and disgust, but I felt hands on the back of my head. Strong hands. Dan's hands, pinning my open mouth to his lover's groin. Above me, I heard his voice.

"Lick Jacklin!" He said it with great force, and he pushed me into her. My tongue began to move out of a combination of survival instinct and a perverse desire. Soon I, was licking his cum out of my wife's pussy hungrily. Greedily. She moved and wiggled and pushed against my face and after a very long time, she signaled him and he released me, and I could breathe again, and I rose, and she leaned against the bed's headboard. Looking up, I saw her smile. She looked happy but exhausted. Dan leaned into her, and they embraced and kissed as I watched.

"As usual, no orgasm," She told him, then to me she said, "No worries honey. Dan made me cum twice before you came in." She then turned back to her lover and said, "Thank you, darling." They kissed again after which both looked at me.

"You should thank him too," Diane told me. She wasn't joking. Both watched me with what I saw as expectancy. Then she elaborated.

"Thank Dan for giving me multiple orgasms. Thank him for doing for your wife what you can't," she said it and I winced, but I could tell it wasn't a request. Dropping my eyes, I cleared my throat and began to speak.

"Uh uh," Diane said as if correcting me. "Eyes up. He's a real man. Look at him and show him the respect he deserves."

I lifted my head slowly and Dan's face came into view. He was grinning ear to ear. Then after delaying if I felt was safe, I spoke.

"Thanks for giving Diane multiple orgasms," I said as I looked into his dark eyes.

"And . . . who is Diane . . .?" He asked leadingly.

"My wife," I answered.

"Then don't you think you should include that when you thank me.?" He replied.

I organized my words and began again.

"Thank you for giving my wife multiple orgasms," I said as he watched closely my discomfort.

"And . . . why, do I need to do that, pray tell?" He was getting into his groove, mocking me actively. Meanwhile, Diane chuckled softly but otherwise listened quietly. I coughed slightly. The words stuck in my throat.

"Because . . . I can't." He smiled broadly at my admission.

"Then," he continued "Shouldn't that be part of it?"

"Yes," I agreed. Anything to get this torture over.

"Then, make it so," Dan responded.

"Thanks for giving my wife multiple orgasms . . . Because I can't," I said it with a sense of resolution, hoping the admission would end the ordeal, which had been made worse because I had a lingering taste of his cum in my mouth.

"Sir," he added as the final dagger. I swallowed hard and what went down wasn't more of Dan's ejaculate. It was what was left of my pride. I knelt on my own bed in women's underwear after licking another man's cum from my wife's pussy and thanking him for the privilege of both. What more did I have left? What else could I lose by full compliance? So, I said what was expected as expected, and saw the triumph in his eyes.

"Thank you for giving my wife multiple orgasms, because I can't do that . . . Sir." After I said "Sir" I heard my dear wife snort derisively. Dan's smile broadened which I would have not believed possible. I hoped his face would crack, but it did not.

After they were satisfied, they had debased me enough, I was dismissed.

"Go into the hamper," Diane told me, "And get the pair of panties I had on. You can wear those today."

I rummaged through the dirty laundry and found my wife's soiled underwear. As I started to exit, he stopped me.

"What do you say to your wife? For letting you wear her dirty panties?"

I was looking directly at Diane I spoke.

"Thank you for letting me wear your dirty panties," I said humbly.

"Ma'am," Dan said correcting me.

"Thank you for letting me wear your dirty panties, Ma'am," I said it while looking at them both and I saw the contempt in his eyes. Surprisingly enough, I saw it in her eyes too.

"Now go away." He said to me brusquely as Diane buried her beautiful face in his chest again.

So, I left the bedroom. Our bedroom and went to the spare. Before my head hit the pillow another text dinged in . . .

Coffee at 9:30 Breakfast at 10.

Knock before you come in

Good night Jacklin

I didn't reply. I merely lay on top of the covers and stretched out, trying to absorb what had just happened. How my life had become such a nightmare. Then, in the room I had just left I started hearing sounds. It started with laughter and grew into crescendos of moans, screams, and cries both passionate and joyous. As the volume of their sexual expression grew so did my desire and indeed my erection, and I stroked enthusiastically. Despite the humiliation, I had endured, I was less crushed than I was excited and aroused. I pounded my cock faster and harder and as the sounds of love from the next room reached its climax so did I, and I exploded onto the sheets as I collapsed limp and numb as I quickly drifted off into a deeply profound sleep. My shame and fear for the moment put aside.

13

S ATURDAY AFTERNOON I WAS TRAIPSING THROUGH THE AISLES of the grocery store getting what was needed for the Sunday get together we had planned. One last opportunity to use the backyard before the onset of winter. My three kids couldn't attend, and they were really all the family I had left, but Diane's mother and her sister and a cousin said they could make it, though the sister's husband was out of town and would not attend. Secretly, I was glad. I didn't care for him. He was one of those guys who thought he was a hotshot because he was highly placed in a local company and on the fast track. His wife, Diane's sister didn't like me either, but I could avoid her easily enough. I would be busy doing all the cooking and food prep while Diane attended to the harder task of performing as hostess. The group would be rounded out by several mutual friends most of whom were couples. So, I was shopping for under 20 people. I could not have been more confident Dan the man would not be among them. As I had laid in bed that morning, I agonized as to whether Dan would vacate before our guests arrived. As I thought about it, it made no sense that Diane would leave herself open to exposure to her family and our friends.

Dan was an exciting dalliance. Her mother would be there, and my wife, a trained attorney who was much too savvy to take such risky chances. I'd been informed after I cleared the dishes from the breakfast in bed, I had served them that they would be going out dancing that night and would be back late. She could have another night of fun and hustle him out the door in time to avoid any unintended exposure to those who would know little about Hot wifeing and would approve of it even less.

By the time I got done, it was late afternoon and I drove back to my house to unload the groceries and have a moment to myself before Diane found other chores for me to do. As I turned down our street, I noticed something was different from when I left. Dan's car was gone. That fact made me wonder if they had already left for the evening. Or this was my thinking positively, just maybe he had left in advance. Never too early to get a head start on being gone before the party. As I swung my SUV into my drive, I thought how nice it might be to have a Saturday night with my wife. I would even change out of the blasted thong she had given me to wear the night before. As I clicked the remote for the garage door, I was already thinking where I might take her for dinner. Then as the door raised my hopes lowered, then fell, then crashed as I saw the reason Dan's car was not in my drive. It was in my garage, in my space next to Diane's car, and while the garage was a three car, the third bay was still filled with furniture from Diane's old house left there after she moved in three years earlier. Him being in my space meant there was no place I could park except in the drive. Once again, they had me on the outside, effectively blocked out.

So, I parked and started bringing bags in the house through the front door, putting them on the kitchen counters, and going back for more. Looking outside I saw my wife and her boyfriend sitting on the glider. Our glider. The one we bought to watch our grandchildren (when we had them) play in the large, manicured space behind our house. They were talking and enjoying the late afternoon sun in a leisurely fashion while I was hauling in pork chops and slabs of ribs and tubs of potato salad and cases of beer for a party that was for her family, as well as our mutual friends. I was cranky, and worst of all my thong was chafing between my cheeks. Also, the fact that my cock wasn't big enough, so the infernal thing felt binding was annoying the shit out of me.

Then, looking outside, I saw something that was much more than annoying. It was downright disturbing. Dan and Diane were still in the glider, still enjoying the late afternoon sunshine. Though at one point they may have been sitting and talking, Diane most certainly was not. In our backyard, in the glider we had bought to watch the grandchildren we might someday have, my loving wife had her head in her lover's lap giving him a leisurely blowjob. The shock was so great I dropped the bottle of wine I had been holding and it shattered on the kitchen floor. The noise from the crash was so loud, Diane's head jerked up, but quickly pushed back down to Dan's groin by the man himself.

I was still wiping up the splattered wine when Dan and Diane came into the house.

"You need to be more careful, Jacklin," Dan said curtly as I mopped the floor glad what I was cleaning was a chardonnay and not merlot, and praying to God not too many neighbors, had witnessed my wife publicly servicing her lover in our normally quiet suburban neighborhood. Diane giggled at Dan's remark as though it were genuinely funny. Bending down, he kissed her and said, "I'm gonna go hit the head." He then exited down the hall. Once he was gone, I turned to my wife.

"Isn't that what you just did?" The sarcastic remark prompted a derisive snort from her as she then responded, "What's the matter, Jacklin, panties in a wad?" Then she pointed to a place on the floor. "You missed a spot. Get on your knees to get it. You can clean it with your tongue. You're good at that." Then, having lobbed a "snark grenade" at me, she followed her Bull's path out of the kitchen.

Everything was in its place, and it was over an hour later when next I saw Dan and Diane. He was trendily dressed in what was considered a stylish suit for younger men, but which when I saw someone wearing one, I always thought it had been purchased in the boy's department and two sizes too small. What Diane was dressed in also seemed too small, but by three sizes in her case. She came in tugging it and what was apparent was she could pull it up and keep her bosom covered or down and keep her butt cheeks covered. She could not, however, do both.

"I need you to move your car, Jake," Dan told me, and I remembered I was still parked in the drive, behind my space in the garage. The space his car now occupied. My initial impulse was to declare "that's TOO BAD," and stick out my tongue childishly.

But I didn't. Getting my keys, I went out and moved my vehicle out of the way and sat helplessly as the big man's hot car whisked my wife away, as the neighbors, (many of whom undoubtedly witnessed their backyard show), watched their rapid departure. As I heard his tires squeal as he drove out, I had one grateful thought: At least he didn't call me Jacklin.

Once they were gone, I returned to the kitchen to begin the process of food preparation, which for a barbecue had to be done the day before. The meats were put in marinades to enhance the flavor and side dishes readied as were predinner snacks. Before the process was begun, I tended to the most important detail. I got myself a beer and drank half in two swallows, then I was ready to work. As I got deeply involved in my chefdom the beer lubricated my thoughts and tightened the hold jealousy and shame and fear of discovery had over me. Had any friends seen? Had they pressed their noses against their thermal pane windows and watched as my life sucked another man's cock? Did they notice the man was "bigger" than me? In every way? Did they notice she had been coming and going with him and not with me? What did they think was going on? No matter how dirty and perverse were the conclusions they reached, the truth was more sordid. When this all began it was so Diane could have a "little fun." Now her fun was barreling toward derangement. She was giddily . . . no, deliriously out of control. She was headed toward a cliff and dragging me with her. The only place she wanted us to go together was into a disaster. She was self-immolating in a bonfire of sexual excess.

I finished my first beer and got another. Looking out into the backyard, I thought of sitting outside. On the glider. I decided that was a bad idea. So, I sat down at a stool at the bar and drank my beer, then another, then another. Finally, I switched to scotch, so there would be some beers left for the next day's guests. As my thoughts drifted hither and yon, it occurred to me I was the perfect host. Just ask Danny boy "Can I get you anything, Sir? Beer, wine, scotch, dinner, dessert? My wife? Sure thing. Right away Sir. Help yourself."

I shifted uncomfortably on my seat, as the thought made my cock twitch and engorge which caused a tightening in my panties. The realization disturbed me greatly, so I did what any other maladjusted husband who had allowed his wife to get involved with a younger, bigger, better endowed man would do. I poured myself another drink and sat some more. Sitting and drinking became too easy, so I kept doing it, along with not eating, which I had not done since the Costco hotdog I'd had almost eight hours earlier. It was good and it was cheap, but it wasn't eight hours good and the drinking with nothing absorbing the booze got me increasingly drunk, until, inevitably, I folded my arms onto the bar in front of me and, laying my head on them like they were a pillow, I fell asleep.

Sometime very late that night, or maybe it was early Sunday morning, I felt something tickling my neck. I had sobered up enough to feel it and, thinking it was a fly, brushed at it lethargically with my hand. Then I heard," Hey!" Through my groggy haze, I smelled a familiar scent. It was my wife's perfume. The one I'd given her on her last birthday, along with jewelry and a new car to assuage the pain of turning 40. Then, placing my hand back on the bar, I once more felt the gentle tickling on my neck. It was her lips. I didn't recognize them because it had been so long since I had felt such tenderness.

"Wake up, lazy butt," I heard her say softly. With great effort, I lifted my head and looked at her. More than smiling, she was beaming at me. I grunted a response, which at that point was the best I could do.

"I really, really liked what you did yesterday," she said breathlessly. "I loved you being part of things. Did you like it too?" Unable to speak, I merely nodded in response.

"Good," she replied enthusiastically. "Dan and I agree we want you to be part of things. But" she said giving me a sideways glance. "you have to promise to do exactly what we say. Can you do that?" Still unable to speak, and unwilling to think, I nodded again.

"Goodie," she said eagerly, "now I am going to the bedroom. I want you to bring a bottle of that scotch Dan likes and the ice bucket. Take off all your clothes and leave them in the spare room."

She turned slightly, then looked back.

"You are still wearing my thong, aren't you?" Once again, I nodded in reply, which made her smile and wrapped her arms around me, and hugged me after which we kissed, with some degree of passion, for the first time in what seemed like forever. "Leave that on."

"Oh," she said as she started back to the bedroom "I am so happy and so glad we had this nice talk. Hurry along now. Don't make me wait."

Sitting on the same stool where I had slept, I watched as she walked away, still in the same tight short dress she had left in the previous evening. Watching her walk away was one of life's great guilty pleasures, and I savored it till the door closed. Then, I filled the ice bucket I kept under the bar and then grabbed a bottle of Johnny Walker Blue and headed to the spare room where I hurriedly tore off my shoes, sock, jeans, and shirt. Soon I was naked and picking up the bucket and the bottle and heading to my bedroom, hoping I was not already too late.

"You want me to wear . . . that?" I was astounded and more than that confused. I had put the scotch and the ice on the bureau and turned to the bed and saw my wife holding a small, tubular contraption. Pink and shaped like a little helmet, attached to a ring. On the ring, there was a tiny brass padlock.

"Yes," she replied. She said it very definitely and her definite tone made me cringe slightly. "Look at it? Isn't it cool?" She held it toward me as Dan remained smugly silent. Watching as my wife convinced me to let her lock my cock in a chastity device. The look on his face said he knew there was no chance she would not succeed.

"You want us to have fun, don't you?" She asked in an exasperated tone. "You want me to have fun, don't you?"

Taking it from her, I looked at it, turning it to see it from all angles.

"And, after all . . . let's face it's not like, your little dick Is really useful anyway. How bad could locking it be?"

I stopped examining the device and glared at her after that statement.

"That's harsh," I told her indignantly.

"Just kidding," she said holding up her hands defensively. "Ya know, you used to have a sense of humor." Dan laughed once more at my expense. Harsh or not, funny, or not, at the end of the day, I realized she was right. So, handing her back the contraption, I accepted my defeat.

"Show me how to put it on," I said resignedly. Then she fairly leaped off the bed, pulled her underwear to my ankles, and did just that. Soon my member was not only tiny but hidden completely away from polite society in its pink prison.

"Why pink?" I had to ask.

"Why not?" Dan answered. "It's mine. Oh, I don't wear it . . ."

"It would never fit you," Diane interrupted. "Though on you," she said speaking to me, "it's kinda big." The comment made me frown and Dan grin.

"I've used it on other husbands," he explained. His explanation and the idea that what was on my genitalia had been on the genitals of others prompted me to look at both with alarm. Dan "eased" my concerns.

"The cage is dishwasher safe," he told me. "Sanitized, for your protection."

Then, after giving me one last look of satisfaction, she turned back to her lover.

"Now, my darling . . . where were we? Oh yes," and with that statement, she embraced him, and they kissed, till she momentarily glanced back my way.

"Put the panties back on," she ordered me, and she pointed to the corner, where a new piece of furniture had been added. A chair. Metal, with a vinyl seat and a, straight back. It did not match the decor, but that wasn't the intent. It matched the spirit of the acts they had planned and my place in the scheme of things. I learned that night about what was called a "Cuckolds chair."

So then, after I pulled the small lacy garment over my entrapped member she told me, "Sit."

She slipped the small tight dress over her head, and I realized she was naked underneath. Once it was off, she was bare except for the matching heels which she left on as she went to work unbuckling Dans belt. His suitcoat was off already, and his dress shirt fully unbuttoned revealing his well, developed chest. As fast as she could work, she had him stepping out of his suit pants and standing in front of her in his boxer briefs, a manly bulge protruding toward her enticingly. Looking at it, she licked her lips and taking hold of the waistband of the black stretchy briefs, drew them down his hips till his long cock sprang free. Though I'd seen it more than once, each time it was an impressive sight. Dropping to her knees she devoured him like a delicious meal, his cock going in and out of her hungry mouth, amazing me with how much of it she could take. Finally, she released it from between her lips and she got back on the bed, crawling backward till she was against the headboard, where she lay propped up and grinning. As I watched in morbid fascination he got on the bed too, kneeling with his monstrous weapon pointing at my wife, waiting. Waiting for . . . what? Still staring at her lover, Diane spoke to me.

"Dan's cock," she explained impatiently. "Put it in me. Please help me," She asked, "Please. I need you."

I sat frozen, and nobody else moved, as Diane pleaded with me again.

"Please . . ."

I moved as if I were in a dream, watching from outside myself as I got out of the chair and joined my wife and her lover on our bed. Her laying with her legs splayed and waiting. Him kneeling with his hard and throbbing member still dripping the saliva of the woman I loved. Slowing, fearfully, I reached out, touching Dan's monster cock with only my fingertips. Meanwhile, somewhere very far away, I heard Diane's voice.

"Yes!"

Dan moved his hips as I guided him to my wife's hot and waiting pussy. The head was at her lips, and he was shoving into her when simultaneously both waved me away and I jumped back, as though I had thrown an explosive charge into a coal mine. It made me want to scream, "Fire in the hole!" I didn't, but there was, and in seconds they were fucking with a ferocity that was frightening. The bed shook and more. The room seemed to come apart around me on a level that could only be measured on the Richter scale. I stood and stepped back to avoid becoming collateral damage. They no longer knew I was there, that I was watching. In this seismic event, there was only them. They were each other's whole world. Then, finally, they screamed in unison, signaling their shared orgasms exploding like the finale of the wildest fourth of July display I had ever imagined.

Then, like a freight train reaching the station, they slowed gradually, finally stopping, and he rested his weight on her inert body until finally, he raised himself off her and pulled out, his now flaccid cock dripping their shared juices, trailing strings of cum across the sheets. Finally, Diane roused out of her catatonic state and looked at me grinning weirdly. Then, pointing at her slimy, reddened pussy she said to me, "Your turn."

Slowly, I crept up between her spread legs and buried my face in her gleaming snatch, licking and sucking as if my life depended on it, and as I did, she began to respond. To make sounds. Sounds I recognized from before. Before hot wifeing, before Dan, before her cunt had been ruined for me by his behemoth. They weren't primal like the ones I heard while they fucked. They were softer, gentler, but they were there. She was making them and as my tongue continued its work they grew and soon I knew she was once again in the throes of orgasm, and I was causing it. That realization made my cock swell and push against its pink prison. As she entered the final stages of climax, she gripped my hair and held me to her and cried out and then, once again, went limp, as Dan sat on the bed watching us. Finally, he was the one left out.

But not for long, once she regained her senses, Diane looked at her lover then looked at me and pointed at Dan's wet and slippery cock, which was now in recovery mode from having witnessed the interaction of his woman with another man. As she pointed, she spoke to me, directed me.

"His turn." I knew what she meant. I didn't like it, but I knew, and I desperately wanted to please her. So, I reluctantly turned to the big man. To his hardening cock, growing more quickly by the second. Then I looked back at my wife, who smiled and gave a small, but enthusiastic nod of encouragement. So, I tentatively placed the head to my lips and gave it a tiny kiss. Behind me, I heard my wife giggle joyfully, so I kissed it more fully and she sighed. Then I took it in my mouth and whatever other sounds she made were drowned out by the thunderous drumbeat of my heart, pounding like a triphammer as I swallowed his mammoth shaft and began to suck, cleaning both their juices off it, but also thereby encouraging a fresh flow. He was cumming in my mouth. Tasting his cum secondhand was nothing compared to experiencing it in all its warm freshness as it came in strong and heavy spurts. I wanted to pull off. I tried, but he held me tightly to his groin and I swallowed mostly out of self-defense until finally, it stopped, and he released me, and I pulled my head up to see my wife watching. Her face looked odd. Her expression a mixture of amazement, glee, and revulsion. Her smile was strange and frozen, and her index finger went to the corner of her mouth and pointed. Reaching up, I realized a dribble of semen had escaped and so I wiped it away which elicited a small nod. Then as if resentful of our silent communication, Dan got between us and took Diane in his arms and kissed her powerfully and deeply and for a long time. Then, he summarily dismissed me, and my wife sat silently as I slunk out of the room, still locked. On my way to the spare bedroom, I stopped in the hall bath to throw up.

Later as I lay in the small bed unable to relieve myself, the taste of his essence mingled with the taste of vomit, self-hatred, and shame in my mouth. I slept little and when I did drift off the sleep was fitful and filled with nightmares of what I had done and what I was willing to do in the name of love.

14

THAT MORNING, HAVING PLACED THE MARINATED RIBS in the smoker to begin the slow process toward their becoming dinner, I drank coffee and began to mentally list priorities to be ready for our guests. Priority number one on the list was getting my wife's "Boy Toy," packed and out the door. Number one A was getting the constricting hunk of metal out from between my legs. As I thought and the caffeine kicked in the priorities changed in their order of importance depending on whether my sense of shame was engaging, or my cock was engorging. What I knew at my core was that neither the cage nor the boyfriend could be present at today's gathering of family and friends.

"Good morning." Diane had come up quietly behind me, barefoot and wrapped in her fluffy robe. She ran her hands through her hair sleepily and yawned, then pulling a cup off the rack placed it in front of me. The expectation was I would pour it for her. Which I did, and fix it as she liked it, which I also did, handing it to her meekly.

"Is he still sleeping?" I asked. The question caused her to frown slightly.

"I'm out here, aren't I?" She responded. "If he were awake, would I be out here?"

It was a valid point, but I didn't tell her that.

"He is going to leave before our guests arrive, isn't he Diane?" The question seemed so obvious, I felt foolish asking it, but Dan's continued presence made me increasingly nervous. She took another sip of coffee and looked at me with a small enigmatic smile. Then, placing her cup on the counter she reached between my legs and felt the hard plastic cage she had locked there. The discovery caused her smile to widen.

"It's still there, huh?" She moved her hand away and drank more coffee.

"Unlock me, Diane," I asked, "You have the key, don't you?" I prayed she had it and not him. Reaching into the pocket of her robe, she brought out the key and held it in her palm so I could see it.

"Take it," she told me. "If, you really want it that is." She looked at me knowingly and continued. "You could have broken out. The padlock is small." My freedom was so close. All I had to do was take it. Why could I not? She knew the answer. So, did I. I didn't respond, didn't comment. Her question was a good one. Why had I not? We looked at each other and she nodded as if she knew why. I knew too, in places within myself I couldn't acknowledge to anyone, much less to myself. She however completed my unfinished thought.

"A real man would have broken out," She stated flatly. "But then a real man would have never been caged."

With that hanging in the air, she turned and walked away, back to the bedroom, carrying her coffee. Then stopping, she turned back and looked at.

"Dan needs a cup of coffee," she said, "Remember three sugars. You can bring yours too . . . if you want him to add some cream that is."

15

"DIANE'S BRAGGED ON YOUR RIBS," Dan told me as I cleared away the tray from the breakfast in bed, I had served him and my wife. "I can't wait to taste them."

"Well, it's only fair," Diane said to him, "After all, he's tasted your bone, darling." She laughed as she said it and then they kissed, and I carried the dishes out. Once I was in the kitchen a text from Diane beeped in.

Come back We forgot something

Motivated by curiosity but also afraid, I loaded the dirty dishes in the dishwasher and returned to the bedroom where my wife and her lover stood, fully naked. Him stretching his sinewy frame and her rummaging through her drawer.

"Here," she said as she handed me a small white scrap of satiny fabric. I held it up, looked at it, and recognized it as one of her thongs. "I chose white in case you wear those awful white shorts I hate." Though I looked at her blankly, my traitorous dick pushed against its pastel prison. She then made a sweeping motion with both hands.

"Now, go . . . shoo . . . get dressed!" She said dismissing me. "We have guests coming and you have things to do."

Trudging toward the spare room, a couple of things were clear. One was Dan wasn't leaving. The other was that she would not be unlocking me anytime soon. If I wanted out, she had told me what I could do, and we both knew I wouldn't do it. So, I stopped in at the hall bath and sat to pee. Then putting on my new underwear, I headed to get dressed.

As it turned out, the white thong was a good choice since it didn't show under my white shorts. Plus, the shorts were tight enough that the cage gave me a nice bulge I would not ordinarily have had. Chastity wasn't as bad as it seemed.

Diane wore a sundress that was cute and tasteful and not of the obscenely low cut or short variety Dan seemed to favor. Seeing her in it led to speculative thoughts as to what (if anything) might be underneath. I was no longer sure whether I would be allowed to find out, so speculation was all I had. Dan, (finally) emerged in jeans and motorcycle boots and a very tight t-shirt that accented his musculature. They stood together just outside the backdoor. Diane looking at Dan lasciviously. Dan watching me work. Neither offered to help. I had the situation well in hand and, Dan quickly had my wife well in hand, and seeing it I cringed fearing a friend or relative showing up unexpectedly early.

Luckily, everyone came on time or slightly late, except for Diane's sister Dana, who though usually late, was half an hour earlier than I'd been told she'd be there. She came alone, as her husband Sean was in San Francisco on business and had been all week. I met Dana at the door and was dismissed as Diane's younger sister rushed through the house to the backyard. The sisters greeted each other with the air kisses women do, and then my wife went to introduce her sibling to her lover.

"And, this must be Dan," she exclaimed in delight. "I have heard so much about you," Then she gathered him in her arms and embraced him warmly, which was more than she had done for me in three and a half years, and that was even after I paid for her bridal shower two years earlier. Once she had released

Dan from her stranglehold, Dana took her sister by the hand and dragged her toward the house. As they walked away the word, I heard was . . . "Details!" Diane and her sister kept little from each other, so I had no doubt, Dana got as many details as were possible before the other guests began straggling in.

"This is my friend Dan" Became the standard line of the day or a variation, "This is Dan. He's, my friend." Then, as a special treat, "Mama, you just have to meet Dan," When my mother-in-law finally arrived accompanied by her hugging him and kissing his cheek, after which she waved and said hello to me in an embarrassed fashion. I got even. I called her Sheila and not mom. Throughout the afternoon Diane was rarely away from Dan's side and they ate together. There were never inappropriate which had been my fear. There was an intimacy to their interaction that had to tell our friends and family . . . "something." I missed my kids not being there, but in a way I was grateful. They were grownups and would have been supportive but embarrassed for me. It would have increased the emotional pain of the day, which was deep and profound already. I got through it and as the barbecue was eaten and the beers drunk the guests left as well until finally, it was Dan, Diane, and Dana sitting in lawn chairs and chatting happily as I cleaned up the mess.

"Jack," Diane called to me. "Come here a minute please." As I walked away from the grille, I heard the two women giggling and felt a certain suspicion and indeed fear creep in as I got closer. As I stood waiting to learn why I had been summoned, the laughter became more raucous. and Dan joined in the chorus.

"Diane told me about," Dana pointed to the front of my shorts, and I blushed a deep red.

"She did . . . WHAT?" I exclaimed in outrage that I am sure could be heard two streets over. Both women placed their index fingers to their lips and went "Shhhh." Dan merely laughed louder.

"How could you?" I asked my wife plaintively. She was still laughing as she got up off the glider where she'd been seated beside Dan and hugged me in a sisterly way.

"Poor baby," She said as she continued the passionless embrace. "You know I tell Dana everything." That statement made the sisters giggle more, with Dana adding, "And she told me EVERYTHING," and she winked at me after she said it.

"She wants to see . . . it," Diane whispered into my ear.

"NO," I said as definitely as a husband can after his cock has been locked up by his wife.

"Don't you want to make me happy?" She cooed, "I promised Dana. You don't want to make me break my promise, do you?" She gave me her best fake sad face and stuck out her lower lip in a pout. I tried the NO one more time, but by then, it sounded less like an exclamation than a plea, and a pathetic plea at that. She batted her eyes at me, and I knew I was done.

"Okay," I said reluctantly. "Let's go inside."

"Inside?" Dana said in protest. "I hear there are lots of things that go on out in the backyard here." More laughter. "You have the privacy fence," she added. "I'm pretty sure no one would climb that high fence to get a look at you parading your shortcomings around the neighborhood."

"C'mon, honey," my wife said encouragingly. "Open your shorts. Let sissy see." My hand moved to my fly, and I unzipped. Looking around self-consciously, I parted the fly. When I did Dana shrieked.

"What the fuck?" She cried as she saw what I was wearing. As she said it, she jumped off the glider, undid my belt, and unbuttoned my shorts, in one motion. Once they were undone, she yanked then to my ankles, and I stood almost naked from the waist down.

Almost.

"A THONG???" She virtually screamed in delight. "Oh how, PRECIOUS!" Reaching out, she touched the satiny fabric. Once she had fondled it to her satisfaction, she moved it aside so she could see the cage.

"Ooooooooh," she said, sounding impressed. She took her index finger and moved it around to get a look at it from all angles. "I need one of these for Sean for trips."

Diane snorted. "Think you could get him to wear it?"

Dana shook her head.

"Most men won't," Dan interjected.

"Real men won't," my wife added, stabbing me in the heart once more. Dan and Dana laughed as if it was a joke. I however knew it was not.

Having endured as much verbal abuse as I could from the three of them, I pulled up my shorts and left and went back to cleaning the grille. Dan and my wife and her sister sat on my glider a while longer sipping beers and laughing, until, when it finally got completely dark, and the mercury lights came on. Then they went into the house. I had just finished scraping the burned-on residue off the metal grate and my phone clicked in a text.

Are you coming in soon?

It was from Diane, to which I replied:

Yes, I just finished

She responded:

Good Hurry up, we need drinks

Luckily enough I made it to the bar before anyone died of thirst. Diane had vodka with a twist Dan had (of course) Johnny Walker Blue, and Dana had a stinger on the rocks. It was because of my sister-in-law and her drinking habits that I kept a couple of bottles of creme de menthe in reserve. I stayed with beer and went and brought in a fresh one from the cooler outside. By the time I came back in Dan and Diane, who were seated side by side on the sectional and were engaged in vigorously examining each other's larynxes as Dana watched from the other end of the leather couch. The weather had turned cool and so I started the gas fireplace and sat in one of the wingchairs to either side of it. As it turned out I did not need the added warmth. The heat being exerted by my wife and her lover was already making me sweat.

Dana watched in fascination, and I watched in shame as the two lovers put on a display of arduous and creative necking, kissing, and fondling until finally, they succumbed for a moment to the need for air and booze. By then, my beer was gone, and I headed toward the bar to switch to scotch. Dana Held her empty glass toward me which I took to mean she needed of a refill. Having at that point known her for three years I was glad I had a second bottle of creme de menthe in the liquor cabinet.

When I returned with the drinks, Diane's short skirt was hiked up around her hips, and a pair of lacy panties were discarded on the arm of the sectional. As I witnessed the display it dawned on me how my perception of my wife had changed, because what most surprised me was not that Diane had allowed her lover to remove her panties on the couch, in our living room while being watched by her husband and her sister. What surprised me most was that she had been wearing panties at all. Such speculation was interrupted by Dan pulling my wife's light summer top over her head and deftly unhooking her bra, freeing her tits so he could maul them. His mouth was on her hard nipples as she threw her head back in a demonstration of her pleasure, while her lover reached and undid his pants, freeing his massive cock. When it sprang free Dana gasped and gulped her drink, handing me back the empty glass. I held it but did not rush to get her a refill, as much a relief as it might have been to get away. To not have to be a witness to the spectacle of my wife's sexual excess, to not feel my cock harden and push painfully against its restrictive prison. I couldn't help myself. I couldn't not watch as the one I loved once again betrayed all we had once held dear. I couldn't not watch as another man fulfilled her in ways I never could.

Dan flipped her around like a rag doll, turning her so her face was buried in the leather cushions of the couch and her ass was raised and her legs splayed. He entered her from behind and she squealed in glee and her sister gasped again. I on the other hand drew in a long breath and did not let it out again until the pair came, with a raucous abandon that caused their tangled bodies to roll off the couch and finally end up under the cocktail table. It was only then that I retreated to the bar. Dana wanted another drink, and I once again desperately needed one.

As it turned out Dana and I needed two more and so did Dan and Diane, their energies depleted after their amorous activities. Once we had all finished the "two more" I called Dana an Uber and sent her on her way.

"You can get my car back to me tomorrow right Jack?" She asked, weaving slightly as she handed me the keys. "After all," She said looking at Dan and Diane retreating toward my bedroom, "It's not like you have anything else to do." Wincing at the implied insult, I took the keys as a late model Subaru pulled up in front of the house. Before she left, she looked me in the eye, grinning, and said, "Have fun." Then taking hold of my cock cage she shook and it and said," Oh, I forgot . . . you can't." With that, she turned and left, while I went to the spare room and listen to the sounds of love from my own bedroom that both excited and tortured me. Finally, the infernal din created by my wife and her lover died down and I was able to think. A lot had happened in a short period of time, and I tried desperately to sort through it. In many ways, it was like being caught in a swift current, and fighting not to drown. Sunday's party had gone better than I dared hope, with no untoward displays by either Diane or Dan. That was on the good side of the ledger. On the other side, was that Dan had been accepted warmly by our friends and Diane's mother. Dana didn't count. She disliked me, so her accepting another man in her sister's life was a given. Which confounded me, I had never been anything but kind and even generous with her. Maybe that was the problem. She perceived that as a weakness. Our friends and my mother-in-law were more troubling. They all embraced Dan readily and so fully, it made to insecure in ways that Diane's being enveloped by him sexually had not. Suppose this became more than physical. Suppose they were falling in love? The anxieties those thoughts cultivated in me excited me more than I dared admit, even to myself, and as I lay on the small bed alone, my cock twitched in futility.

Thinking of this was wearing me out and exhausted I fell into a troubled sleep, still wondering how it was I was so easily replaced?

16

THE NEXT MORNING, I WAS UP AND READY and driving Dana's car back to her before Dan and Diane left the house, but not before I took them coffee and debased myself by asking and then begging to be unlocked. My wife sipped her coffee and teasingly fingered the key, which was on a chain around her neck as she demurred, saying I should "ask her later." Dan was holding her as he smirked at me, and the smell of sex was still heavy in the room. Hurriedly, I made my exit, and soon I was at my sister-in-law's front door ringing the bell. She answered the door in a short silk robe with oriental symbols. Handing her the keys I turned to leave. She called me back.

"Come in," she said "Let's have coffee and talk." I blinked in surprise at having been acknowledged as something more than a vehicle deliverer or a cocktail waitress. Apprehensive as to her motivation, but also curious about it, I went in, feeling like the proverbial fly, going willingly into the parlor of a very seductive spider.

Once we got to the kitchen, she pushed a mug towards me, and I filled it for myself. Then she pushed the one she had been drinking from and I refilled hers, after which she nodded to a plastic bottle of flavored creamer, and I added some and handed her the mug.

"Thanks," she said as she lifted the sweetened mixture that was once coffee to her lips and took a sip, and then licked the ceramic rim suggestively.

Her breakfast bar had three tall stools. Dana pushed one out so I could sit, then she sat on the one next to it. As she settled in, the robe crept up her legs and I realized that Dana unlike her sister, had not had a Brazilian wax, and the curly strands of her pubic hair were peeking out from beneath the silken fabric. She noticed me looking and smiled.

"So, you're still locked up." It was a statement, not a question. After she said it, she spread her legs a little more, and the robe seemed to get smaller. The sisters had obviously talked. There was nothing I could confirm she didn't already know. So, nodding, I drank some more coffee. It was good coffee, but it could have been gasoline and I would have drunk if only to have something to do besides screaming in sexual frustration.

"Oh," she began, "what must it be like . . . being locked away. So close to a beautiful woman. To be denied." As she said it, she crossed her legs, obstructing what had begun to be a direct view of her pussy. When she did it, the upper part of the robe fell more open, exposing more of her breasts. Wait . . . was that a hint of nipple I saw? I looked away and drank more coffee.

"Then," she continued, "to see that beautiful woman, taken by a man. A powerful man. Used in ways you have only been ever able to dream of, well, that must be torture."

Leaning across to me, she placed a hand on my leg and patted it sympathetically.

"It's terrible, being denied," she continued, "I understand because I'm being denied too," he sat back on her stool and looked and the place between my legs and grinned. "I'm not even locked up."

Picking up her cup, she drained it. Then she held it toward me.

"I'd like some of that, wouldn't you?" she asked enticingly, "Coffee that is."

I sat looking at my beautiful, half-dressed sister-in-law, unable to move. Unable to speak. So, she poured herself another mugful and drank, looking at me intently.

"Dan is, a gorgeous man," she said finally, "With a magnificent cock." After she said it, I sat as still as I could. My paralysis made her laugh.

"Here's the deal," she said, "Diane has this beautiful man, with this magnificent cock, and she is being a selfish bitch with me. That's hardly fair, is it? I mean, she's shared it with you. Why not me?" The fact that she knew made me flinch, which prompted a laugh from Dana "Does it shock you, that I know?" She asked. "Diane tells me everything, and I do mean everything."

I blinked and Dana straightened on her stool and pulled the front of her robe back together.

"Don't worry," she assured me, "I'll tell no one." She then flashed a coquettish smile and added, "Well, almost no one."

She looked at me a long time, trying to make me uncomfortable. It was working, and I felt my inbred "fight or flight" response click into flight and I turned to leave. She grabbed me by my arm and held it tightly.

"I need you, Jack," she said. It was not a request; it was an expectation. I was getting a lot of that from the women in my life lately. "You need to talk to Diane." She appeared to be adopting what was called a "doe-eyed" appearance, which I knew was fake, but which I also know worked for her with men, and I was no exception. As she spoke, she pulled me in closer, as if to emphasize an intimacy I knew we didn't have, but that was working too.

"You must be so . . . desperate," she told as if we were sharing a secret. "I understand. I'm desperate too. Sean's gone all the time, and he comes home too tired to . . ." her eyes went away from mine theatrically as she said, "well, you know." I nodded slightly, though I didn't know. I was sure I had never been so physically exhausted. Under endowed doesn't mean under enthusiastic. Being in such proximity to a woman as sexy a Dana hadn't served to dampen that enthusiasm and my "little soldier" was knocking at the door of his cell, insistent on a release my "other head" knew was not to be. Watching as she opened her robe fully and ran her hands down her ripe young body, from breasts to pussy and back again. definitely, not helping my situation, but I got the feeling my sister-in-law didn't care. In fact, I knew by then that was her plan.

"You help me," she said in a breathy voice, "and I will help . . . you." As I took in the sight of her stroking her body, watched her nipples stiffen and a glistening sheen form on the lips of her unshorn pussy, I nodded some more then finally, finding my voice I asked:

"How?"

Dana's lips formed a wolfish smile knowing I was taking the bait.

"We can discuss that after you have helped me in . . . 'another' way." She scooted her ass to the edge of her stool, opened her robe, and parting her legs as wide as was physically possible. Then she pointed suggestively to the space on the floor in from of her. I knew what she was suggesting and tried to fight the urge. My sexual deprivation overcame my sense of propriety and I got off my seat and knelt before her. Above me, I heard her chuckle slightly.

"My sister tells me you are as good with your tongue as you are . . . 'limited' with your cock," she said derisively. "Show me those skills and then we can figure out how to get that wife of yours to be a little less selfish."

17

SHOW HER I DID. THREE TIMES IN FACT, after which she collapsed onto the stool in a limp heap. My own tumescence remained unrequited, a fact that concerned her not at all.

"You do realize," Dana began after she regained her senses. "That it's in your best interest split Dan's attentions, right? It seems to me in watching Diane and talking to her, she's falling in love with him."

I listened without comment, but I knew what she said was true. I always knew in the back of my mind that was a danger. Even as my wife reassured me this was a "fling" and purely physical, what I'd seen the previous day and the days before had made me understand that if she wasn't intentionally lying to me, she was lying to herself. The problem had been what could I do about it? Then, it dawned on me the solution had now presented itself, and all it had cost me was an extended session of cunnilingus and several curly pubic hairs stuck in my throat. Dana laughed as I made a choking sound. The tracheal obstruction made me appreciate Diane's recent depilation. Thanks, Dan.

"Sean doesn't care," Dana explained. "He goes down on me as quickly as he can, to get to the 'main event.' Which is also kinda quick. As he always says, 'time is money.'" Then, looking thoughtful, she reached into a nearby cabinet, took out a bottle of brandy, and added a generous portion to her cold coffee. Once that was done, she held the bottle toward me. I demurred. 10:23 a.m. might be cocktail hour for Dana, but it was not for me. At least not yet. She took a long drink of the brandied concoction, and I could almost see the resultant glow of the alcohol mixing with the sexual satiation provided by my tongue. She had her eyes tightly shut and her mouth forming a thin smile, which broadened as she finally spoke.

"So, what's it like to be a cuckold?"

The question stunned me and would have surprised me more from most anyone else besides my wife's sister. Dana took pride in being outrageous and acted out in that manner whenever possible. Which was usually when her husband was out of town, on one of his frequent business trips. Maybe I'd travel frequently too if I was married to a woman like Dana. Then it struck me that my wife's behavior was starting to mirror that of her sister in terms of a callous disregard for my feelings. That made me wonder whether I should consider going back into business in a field where frequent travel was necessary. Which then led me to speculate as to whether my chastity cage would get through airport security. It is amazing how many wild speculations can go through a guy's head when he wants to avoid an awkward question. But Dana was fortified with alcohol and endorphins. She had patience. She could wait. Until, as I finally realized that fact, I answered as best I could.

"Uh," I began haltingly, as my brain scrambled to organize a reply. "The fact is I'm, not a . . . THAT." Dana's slow head nod and "Uh-huh," told me she didn't believe me, so I tried to stammer a further explanation.

"This is really a 'Hot Wife' thing. Diane's the Hot Wife, and well, I'm . . . the 'husband,' and Dan's a fling."

Dana's nodding turned to a headshake as she shook her head indicating disbelief, she took another slug of liquid courage and resumed speaking.

"Your wife is 'hot,' that's for sure." As she spoke, she had dribbled a little brandied coffee down her chin. Taking her finger, she wiped at it and placed the tip to her lips sucked it clean suggestively.

"Dan's her bull," she continued," and you, dear brother-in-law, are their cuckold."

I picked up the bottle and poured brandy into my half-empty cup, till it was a full cup. When I lifted it to my mouth my hand was shaking so badly, I had to steady it with the other. Dana laughed and I wasn't sure if it was because of my obvious nervousness or my absurd situation. I drank more brandied coffee which helped me clarity and decided it was both.

She continued to speak, and I continued to listen, and we both continued to drink as she outlined our shared goals, and her desire to get my wife to share time with her with our "Bull."

"I need access to that beautiful cock," she explained, "and you dear cuckie, need me to have it so he has less time, for Diane. Less energy too," she added shooting me what I interpreted as a lascivious grin and drained her cup as she did so. She was already buzzed, and it wasn't yet 11 a.m. She was riding a high of alcohol-fueled sexual fantasies. All of which involved my wife's lover's ample endowment. Finally, I had heard enough and summoned an Uber. I needed to be alone. I needed to think.

18

I FINALLY GOT HOME A LITTLE BEFORE NOON, with my head spinning. The house was quiet and dark and otherworldly from the space I had come to know the last two weekends. It was as though I was an astronaut, returning to my planet after spending too long on alien worlds, or a time traveler, caught outside his own era, dazed, and confused at having spent too much time trying to avoid being stepped on by mastodons.

Once I got inside, I went to the kitchen. Dishes and glassware and cutlery and serving dishes from the previous day's party were stacked on the counters and in the sink. My fascination with my wife's amorous activities had kept me from doing much of the cleanup a party of that size necessitated. Surprisingly enough, no magical spirits had come in and cleaned up the mess. The fact was, spirits were in the house, but they were inhabiting my wife's formerly sensible brain. Mine too, as I saw myself and her doing things, that not long before, we would have seen as ridiculous, irresponsible, and just plain wrong.

Looking at the mess wasn't helping my head which was pounding, a result of the walking disaster area that my life had become.

Witnessing the multiple debaucheries, the acceptance of abuse, and now diving headlong into a liaison with my sister-in-law involving sexual servitude and complicity in a plot for her to steal my wife's lover. It was all too much, and, unlike Dana, the brandied coffee had not served to aid my thought process. Faced with all that, I did the only thing a man could do. I poured what was left of the morning coffee into a mug, microwaved it, took it to what was apparently now my bedroom, undressed, and lay down on the bed and as I lay there drinking coffee, I contemplated my choices. I was naked except for the thong, which I could have removed easily along with my other clothing, and the chastity device, which I also could have removed but which would have required more effort. I didn't and I was still wearing them two hours later when the coffee was gone. I still didn't understand where I'd gone wrong. Where we had gone wrong. Finally, I reached two conclusions. The first was, I was going to conspire with Dana to help her steal her sister's lover. The second was, Diane and I should have taken up golf.

FINALLY, THE WEIGHT OF ALL THAT EXISTENTIAL THOUGHT was too heavy to carry, so I got up, threw on a pair of sweats to cover the outward evidence of my altered status and a t-shirt, and went to perform the mindless but necessary activity of cleaning the kitchen. After about three hours, the kitchen was acceptably clean, the lawn furniture was stowed, and I had applied leather cleaner to the living room furniture where my wife had dripped her lover's cum. The house looked and smelled clean once again. I felt the pride of a productive house husband, and it was just after five o'clock. I had just sat down when I heard the garage door open. After the weekend, I knew Dan had a garage opener. In fact, I'd parked in the drive so as not to piss off my wife. It was thirty minutes early for her. Fear drove through me with the swiftness of Dan's sports car, burning rubber on my gut as it peeled away. What if it is him? I had never been alone with him and desperately didn't want to be. I was frantically trying to decide whether to hide in the spare room or run outside when I hear a familiar clicking of heels and Diane came in through the laundry room, looking worn slick from too much sexual activity and too little sleep.

"Long day?" I asked because I couldn't think of anything else and wanted to avoid her asking everything I had been doing since she left.

Diane nodded wearily. "Short night, too." She smiled at the memory, and she placed her purse on the counter.

"Can you get me a water, Jack?" She asked and she sat on a kitchen stool placed her arms on the breakfast bar and laid her head on her arms. I placed the water bottle near her and reached over and patted her hair and when my knuckles didn't get rapped, stroked it lightly.

"Let's just stay in tonight," I said. "We can chill on the couch, watch TV, and catch up."

My wife lifted her head sleepily, and with all the energy she could muster, looked at me like I was stupid. I knew the look. I had been seeing it in the mirror for almost two weeks.

"D'uhh," she said mockingly. "Monday Night Football? Remember? "

With all that was going on, I had forgotten. We were scheduled to watch the game with two other couples at a local sports bar, but that was easily fixed.

"Honey," I said sympathetically. "Lets us not go tonight. You are worn out. We can curl up here and you can rest." Her response was to again give me "the look," ratcheted up a notch to "idiot level." I'd seen that one in the mirror too.

"Us?" She said quizzically. "Oh shit . . . Sarah and Jim."

"And Greg and Rhonda," I added trying to jog her memory. "Seven o'clock at Costas."

She put her head back on her arms and said, "I completely forgot."

I tried to put a hand on her head again. This time she swatted it away.

"Dan's having some friends over," she said, her voice muffled because her face was still buried on her forearms. No wonder the us was a question. Then, she raised her head, so I could see her eyes. The look I got this time didn't make me feel stupid, or like an idiot. This time she needed me.

"Can you make my excuses for me, honey?" It was her soulful look. Practiced and effective. "You can still go. Say I had a client or something. Please?"

I looked at her skeptically, but in the end, her look triumphed over mine, and as much as I didn't want her to go to Dans, I knew I couldn't stop her, and I also knew I didn't want to watch the game alone. So, I agreed, I would go and lie to our friends while she would meet him. Seemed like the least I could do.

Apparently not. As soon as I agreed, she jerked her head up and jumped off her stool.

"Here," she said. "Come help me get ready. I'm supposed to be there at 7 and I do not want to be late."

Having noticed the time, she suddenly seemed energized. She kicked off her high heels and ran through the kitchen abandoning the now unneeded footwear, secure in the knowledge I would retrieve them and put them where they belonged, in piles in her closet along with all their sisters.

"Come on," She urged me impatiently. "I have a new outfit and you're going to make me late."

The "new outfit" was a cheerleader's uniform, including the tight lowcut top, ultra-short skirt, and tall, high heeled boots. Oh, and pom-poms.

"Rah, Rah," she said, as she shook her pom-poms and her tits simultaneously. She smiled with more pride than she had when she won that big case against the local power company. Life is all about context. The outfit was tight, but also brief. What fabric there was, was stretchy so we squeezed her into it. Then after she was dressed, she applied fresh makeup and she was out the door at 6:15 to make the 35-minute drive and a dash up the elevator to be at what she called his "Top floor penthouse" exactly on time. She had been there once (that I knew of), and she described it as amazing with a breathtaking view of the city. All I knew was it had another view my lovely suburban house didn't have. A view of my wife. I wallowed in self-pity a while and then got dressed so I could be at Costas by game time and tell our friends a lie they wouldn't believe, so I could bask in their pity and be humiliated once again. This time more publicly. The thought made my cock twitch, which reminded me. Before I would help my wife expedite her departure, I struck a bargain. She had left me the key. I used it to unlock the padlock, and, in a few seconds, my small but turgid package was free. As instructed, I took the device, the lock, and key and put them in the drawer of the nightstand on her side of the bed, (though it seemed like her side of the bed was now right in the middle of Dan's beefy frame). Pulling up my jeans, I readjusted the thong panties, which I had left on because they had started feeling pretty, damn good. Then I pulled on my authentic game-worn jersey and tucked it in. I had no idea how many people had told me that only "dorks" tuck in their jerseys. I did it anyway because for one thing "dork" was often an apt description for me. I wasn't so fat that my belly lopped over my belt, and it was my theory that only fat guys let their shirts hang out of their pants. I tucked it in and headed to be among people who however they might silently judge me for being cucked by my wife knew my name wasn't Jake or Jacklin.

19

"A CLIENT? SO LATE?" SARAH'S POINTED QUESTION reflected the skepticism I had expected to encounter. Did my tissue thin "Lie as explanation" make her more skeptical? Did the fact that she and her husband had been at our Sunday barbecue, had seen Diane with Dan? Undoubtedly. I was lucky, by the time I got there the game had started and my friends were more interested in the plays up on the screen than where Diane was. I on the other hand was not distracted by the gridiron action. My thoughts were elsewhere. In a penthouse downtown with a spectacular view of the city, and an even better view of my wife. My distraction was made worse as questions became more numerous as half time approached and our team behind, though not by a lot.

"Can I get you another beer, Jack?" Looking up, I realized a waitress who served Diane and me frequently. Smiling, I nodded.

"Sure Becky," I replied. She wrote on her pad.

"Where's Missus Jack tonight?" she asked innocently.

"Working," I answered simply.

"Busy girl," she said smiling.

"You have no idea." Why the hell did I say that I asked myself after I said it. Becky paid no mind to what could have been an awkward statement had she been cursed with more information than my choice of beverage. She said, "Mm Hmm," and quickly moved on to the others in our party. Once she had everyone's orders she passed me at a fast walk headed to the bar.

"Well, tell your wife we missed her," Becky said as she flew past, "When you see her."

Looking at the phone, I wondered when that would be. So as the halftime analysis of the game droned on, I messaged.

Good game huh

I waited several seconds and after getting no response, I messaged again.

Close

Again, nothing. I was still staring at my phone when, Jim came over.

"Come over here," he whispered as the second half was getting ready to start.

"Let's go outside for a minute." Wordlessly, I followed him through the crowded bar to the outdoor patio, which was empty except for three people smoking. Once we were out, in the cold, his serious look told me he suspected what I feared.

"Hey," he began carefully, "we've been friends a long time, right?" I nodded in silent agreement. Jim and Sarah were among the few friends I still had from when I was married to Elizabeth.

"I never butt into your business," he continued, "even during the divorce."

I nodded again. Silence was the best I could do at that point.

"But I have got to ask," As he tried to form the words, I already knew what was coming. "What the fuck is going on? What we saw yesterday . . . that wasn't right."

I didn't respond immediately, but I smiled a small bitter smile. All I could think was if he only knew. If he'd only seen. Seen what happened after everyone left. Seen what had been going on for too long. How shocked would he be then?

"What do you mean Jim?" Having no other tactic to evade the

questions that naturally arise when a wife takes a boyfriend to a public event. I decided to play dumb. Jim shoved his hands in his pockets and looked at me blankly. It was cold enough the tactic might just work. He said in exasperation. "Who the fuck is he, and why was he so handsy with your wife?" Jim's mention of Diane caused me to reflexively check my phone. Still no response.

"He's a friend," I explained lamely "We met him at the gym." Jim looked at me questioningly realizing, as did I that the "we" made what I had said less than credible. Sometimes evasion is the best defense. Jim seemed willing to let this drop. Less because he believed me than because his lips were turning blue.

"So," He said as his teeth began chattering, "all is well?"

"Nothing I can't handle," I replied. I had told myself that so much, I almost sounded believable when I told my old friend.

"Good," he said and reached for the door handle. "Cause I'm freezing my nuts off, but Sarah wouldn't give me a moment's peace till I asked." Thanking my friend for his concern we went back into the bar, where blessedly it was warm but also too loud to speak. I was relieved of the burden of easing my friends' minds with something I knew was a lie.

Time passed and the game progressed. Our team won, and it wasn't close. The other couples in my little group left. The wives giving me comforting hugs, while the husbands gave me pitying looks. I stayed and sat, watching the post-game rehash, drinking water, and wondering what Dan was doing with my wife. The truth was, I was afraid to go home. To an empty house, or worse yet, to a house where they had come back to after the game. Her staying with him all night was unlikely. She had to be at the office at 9 a.m., and the likelihood of Diane getting up early enough to drive across town, clean up and dress as impeccably as she always did and get to work on time seemed remote. No, they would come back to my house, perform their satanic rituals multiple times, and be ready for coffee and breakfast delivered in servile fashion by yours truly. So, I sat drinking water until finally post-game gave way to SportsCenter and it was last call. I was sitting at the bar by then and was alone there except for one other patron. A woman who looked to be about my age, 50 something. Attractive with a soft gentility I found engaging after what I'd been through with my supermodel glamorous wife. Looking down the bar, a smiled and she smiled back. It was a sad smile, and it made me wonder if mine was too. I turned back to my water. When I looked up again, she was smiling at me again, so I thought, "What the hell," and moved to the bar to the stool beside hers. Misery loves company, and I was still afraid to go home. Maybe if I stalled long enough, they'd be catching a couple of hours of sleep before their morning couplings.

"I'm Jack," I said never at a loss for a pickup line. Then I pulled out the always trite, "Do you come here often?"

"Hi Jack, I'm Bridgette." She said ignoring my lameness. "No, I don't go out much, and this is new."

"Like it?" I asked because lameness seemed to be working for me here. I decided to go with it for a while. We chatted a while as I drank my water and Bridgette nursed a Chardonnay. The wine and the loneliness caused her to open up about her husband leaving her. I judiciously avoided details, even after she noticed my wedding band, which had once meant so much to me but lately was merely a painful gold reminder. The more Bridgette opened up the more she drank, and "last call" became, "one for the road," allowed, because Becky was taking care of closing, and by the time she kicked us out the door, I was sober, and Bridgette was far too drunk to drive. Despite that, she fumbled for her keys as I walked her out to the parking lot. Finally, she found them and without much struggle, I took them from her.

"Over this way," I said, and taking her arm I gently steered her to my SUV. As we got closer, she turned slightly and took hold of me, and I thought at that point she might resist. Instead, she drunkenly positioned herself in front of me, and taking me in her arms, held me and kissed me, full on the lips. A passionate, probing kiss. The best kiss I'd had since Diane, and I were having the affair that spelled the end of my marriage. It seemed to last forever and when it ended, I was disappointed. She only broke off long enough for her to regain control of her shaky legs, reinitiate, and quickly we were orally engaged again. Kissing in ways I had only witnessed from afar in the recent past. Finally, she pulled her lips away and collapsed with her head on my chest.

"I think I need a ride home," as her face was still buried in my authentic game-worn, tucked in jersey. I agreed with her assessment of her ability to drive herself.

"Can you take me?" She said pulling her head back slightly. I told her I could.

So, after helping her into the vehicle, I did. She didn't doze off till she gave me her address, which I programmed into the GPS app on my phone. As luck would have it, she lived near to me, so I knew the area well. In 10 minutes, we were sitting in front of her house.

"We're here," I said trying to rouse her. She resisted being roused so I went around and opened the car door. The cold night air woke her, but she was so shaky getting out I knew she would never make it inside. So once I steadied her, she held onto me as we started up her front steps. This time it was me fumbling with her keys, (which were still in my possession) until I found her house key. We stumbled in the door, and I asked her the way to her bedroom. She pointed down a hall to our right and I half carried, half dragged her limp form in the direction she indicated, finally coming to a door through which I saw a bed with a white comforter, trimmed in pink, that I knew had to be Bridgette's. Once I got her on the bed, I was about to leave when she once again came alive. Grabbing me she kissed me again and I kissed her back and soon she had pulled me onto the bed, and we were rolling around together Groping each other in ways I hadn't groped or been groped ever. Finally, we cooled ever so slightly, or we had to come up for air. He looked at me and reached and pulled her sweater over her head and quickly we were both shedding our clothes until finally, she was naked, and I was in only my jeans when she started working my belt buckle, and I froze realizing what I was wearing underneath. She persisted and I thought, "What the hell. It's been fun while it lasted," expecting her to laugh once she saw her knight in shining armor was dressed like the princess bride under his clothes. She pulled my pants down and once she could see the lacy thong, she just stopped and looked, a smile formed, and I steeled myself for the laughter I expected to ensue. Laughter which never came. Her smile broadened, but it was an appreciative smile.

"Oh, I love it," she enthused, and then, she reached and slowly and gently tugged the frilly garment down until my little cock popped out. When she saw it, rather than looking disgusted, she looked as hungry as my wife did when she saw her Bulls' "big hunk of meat." The idea that I would have penetrative sex with a woman who did not think of me as "underendowed" caused my cock to surge and grow. Then I looked at her, saw her gaze, a strange and disturbing thing happened. My once strong erection began to wilt, along with my hopes. Bridgette's once admiring gaze turned to surprise and disappointment. She touched it and began a regimen of stroking, rubbing, and massaging. In the end, it was no use. Finally, I did what I had always done with women, she laid back and I pleased her with my tongue and after a lovely though quiet (by Diane's standards) orgasm. Afterward, we held each other on her bed.

"Was it me?" She asked sorrowfully. I shook my head sadly.

"No," I answered, "It most certainly was not you?"

Taking my hand, she rubbed her fingers across my wedding ring.

"Was it . . .?" Before she could finish the sentence, I stopped her.

"Maybe," I replied, "In a way. It's complicated. Very complicated."

Leaning over, I kissed Bridgette lightly on the mouth got up, out of bed, and dressed. She told me to come back sometime, and we exchanged phone numbers. As we did, I noticed there were no messages from Diane. I got in my car for the short drive home. I did it not knowing if my wife was there or not. Not knowing where my wife was or what she was doing was becoming a familiar feeling, but it wasn't getting any easier.

20

"HI, JACK. THIS IS TRACY, DIANE'S ASSISTANT. It's 10:15. We still haven't heard from Diane. I've texted and left her several voice mails. I haven't heard back from her. Give me a call, please. Thanks."

I listened to the voicemail and the five more that had followed and got increasingly worried.

When Diane hadn't come home, I concluded she had clothes at Dan's and that she would change and go to the office from there. I went from annoyed to concerned when her office made it obvious, she had not come in. When the messages kept coming, I went from concerned to worried and was steaming toward calling the police in a panic when after 11 a.m. my wife showed up.

She looked like she had slept in a dumpster and combed her hair with a meat grinder. Oh, and she was moving with all the ease and grace of a wrecked car. Gone was the cute, extra tight cheerleaders' outfit. In its place, she was wearing baggy sweatpants, a sweatshirt with XL in large block letters across her chest (what I later called to her chagrin, truth in advertising) and she was barefoot. As she made her way slowly and silently past me, I swore I heard her clank as she moved.

"Coffee," she called plaintively as she made her was ponderously down the hall "If you have a shred of humanity, you'll bring me coffee and lots of it "

Then, after brewing a fresh pot, I took Diane the coffee she so obviously needed. She was on the bed, on her back, sprawled out, still fully dressed like a homeless person.

"Ahem," I said subtly signaling my presence. She lifted her head slightly. Just enough so she could see me through her bloodshot eyes.

"Do you want to drink this," I asked, "Or shall I arrange a transfusion?"

Dropping her head back on the bed, she said, "Ha Ha Ha. That's so funny I almost forgot to laugh."

"Almost," I said agreeably. Finally, she lifted herself up so that she was resting on the bed's headboard. When she was set, she reached out. Handing her the steaming cup, I said, "Careful, it's hot." Placing the cup to her lips, she pulled it away quickly after taking a small sip, in the process slopped coffee on the comforter.

"Ow!" She whined, "Shit, that's hot." I suppressed the urge to say I told you so, and instead looked at her with what I hoped was sympathy and compassion. It didn't seem to help as she put her coffee on the nightstand to cool and gave me a look that was sort of frightening.

"Help me off with my clothes, she said and then added, "Please." Seizing an opportunity that had not been afforded much recently, I gently lifted the sweatshirt over her head and off. The first thing I noticed (after noticing she was braless), were the deep purple bruises covering both of her large firm breasts, and what looked like blood blisters, which further examination seemed to indicate were bite marks. I looked at them and suppressed a gasp of surprise and horror. Then, she lifted her legs and I pulled off the sweatpants and what I saw was even more shocking and I did more than gasp, I cried out.

"What the fuck?" The words didn't properly express the outrage I felt from seeing the body of the woman I married looking like it had been mauled by a pack of wolverines. I stopped pulling and so she wiggled the pants off the rest of the way and laid on our bed bruised and naked. Worse yet, her pussy, usually a bright and beautiful pink was an angry red. Sore and raw looking. I touched it. Tenderly, lovingly, gently. Yet still, it caused her to scream, to cry you in pain. I pulled away wondering what I could do . . . what should I do? Call a doctor? Call the police? My instincts said I should call a priest to exorcise the demons that had taken possession of my formerly sensible wife. As I tried to decide a course of action, she rallied slightly and raised up took the coffee cup again and sipped some. It had either cooled enough to drink, or she needed it badly enough she ignored the burn. Pain was obviously something she was willing to accept.

"What time is it?" She asked suddenly rousing out of her half-conscious state.

Looking at my phone, I informed her it was a quarter of 12.

"Tracy's been calling me." I told her. "Have you let her know you're all right?" I had to wonder because she had not let me know. I considered that she might keep others better informed. I was only her husband and therefore less important, or now not important at all.

"Shit!" My wife exclaimed and jumping off the bed she started rifling through the rumpled clothes in which she had arrived home. Finally, finding what she sought she pulled her phone out of the pocket of the sweatpants. I looked at it and realized trying to use it was futile. Apparently, it had been mauled by the same pack of wolverines that had attacked its owner. The screen was shattered, and pieces were missing. The body of the phone was mangled and twisted. Years earlier my oldest child's phone had been run over by a car. Diane's phone was in worse shape. She looked at the phone and looked at me and I handed her my phone. She took it without comment and scanned through it. Then she once again said shit, even more forcefully this time, punched the speed dial, and placed the phone to her ear.

"Tracy?" She said into my phone. "Tracy, it's Diane. No . . . Yes

. . . yes, I'm fine . . . Well, no I am NOT fine. I'm sick . . . been throwing up all night. Messages? No, my phone doesn't work anymore. No . . . no . . . I was puking last night, and it fell in the toilet. Yes . . . yes, his phone works . . . No. I don't know why he didn't. He's an idiot, that's why. You are going to have to reschedule everything for today. No, I can't keep anything down . . . Tomorrow. Absolutely. No matter what I'll be there. Yes, I'll have a phone within the hour. Absolutely. Yes. Thank you, sweety. Bye."

My wife handed me back my phone and I took it and frowned as I did.

"Idiot, huh?" I said to her.

"Thank you for not calling her back and telling her what was really happening," she said almost seeming grateful.

"Kinda hard for me to tell them what was 'really happening' when I didn't know myself," I replied.

"True," she responded nodding. "But you didn't panic at least. Didn't call the police."

Nodding I didn't admit I had considered it but elected to wait.

"What the hell happened Diane?" I was getting angry and figured an explanation was way overdue. She merely shrugged.

"Stuff," was all she said. Stuff???

She threw her broken phone on the floor for me to pick up and reached an arm to me so I could help her to her feet.

"I'll explain later," she told me. "Right now, can you draw me a bath and while I'm soaking go to the store and get me a new phone. Then we can have lunch and I'll tell you all about it."

Once she was standing, however shakily, I went to our bathroom and filled the tub, and when the water was right helped her in and after cautioning her to not drown while I was gone, I left to replace her ruined device, assured of something. That while I might not yet know what had happened, I knew one thing. I might be an idiot, but I was a useful idiot.

21

O N MY WAY TO THE PHONE STORE, a call came in from Dana.

"Good afternoon, Dana," I said after switching the call to hands-free.

"Have you talked to Diane yet?" She asked cutting past the pleasantries. Obviously, she had not tried contacting her sister herself. She was depending on me to do her dirty work. Again the "useful idiot" tag fit.

"I am headed back in a bit to do just that," I replied giving no details. Having now experienced the damage being with Dan had caused, I was hoping I could get my wife to abandon the relationship. If abandonment wasn't an option, she would hand him off. Whatever it took, and the fact I disliked Dana intensely was merely a happy coincidence. I wondered what Sean would do if he found his wife like I'd found mine today? Probably not go buy her a new phone. Did it make me a good husband that I had? Or did it mean I was something else? Something that rhymed with "luck?"

O H, THIS IS A NICE ONE," Diane enthused as she played with her new device. "it's got all my pictures and contacts and apps."

"Having everything in 'the cloud' makes that so much easier." I agreed. Plus, not to mention the fact it made it possible to snoop through my wife's contacts and get Dan's info. Or "Big Dan" as he appeared in her phone. No doubt to differentiate him from two clients and a cousin also named Dan. Getting that was part of the plan I had begun to form. Now I had it to give to Dana in case Diane wasn't willing to do the "handoff." Also, should Diane disappear again, I could call him to find out where she was. For all the good it might do.

It was after three o'clock. I'd made us a late lunch of chicken salad. She had a long bath and was out by the time I returned, wrapped in her fluffy robe, sitting on a barstool, having already poured herself a drink and swallowed a handful of Ibuprofen and assorted pain killers and muscle relaxants leftover from when I had broken my leg little over a year ago. Her hair was in a wet tangle, and she wore no makeup, looking like I thought she might have looked when she was a young girl.

"So," I began, satisfied she was a little drunk and less sore and more relaxed. "What happened Diane?"

She sipped her vodka before answering as if to fortify herself so she could answer. After she swallowed, she spoke.

"Did they win?" She asked innocently. Her response startled me.

"You obviously didn't," I replied tartly.

Reaching up, Diane ran her hands vigorously through her damp hair.

"Oh, but I did," she declared smiling." All the guys said so." Opening her robe, she parted her legs putting her inflamed and tender pussy on display for me to see.

"Dan said this is my 'Gang Bang badge of honor.'"

Gang Bang. The term hit me squarely between the eyes.

"You . . . You . . ." I was sputtering, so outraged that I was unable to speak. Diane noticed my struggles and courteously finished the sentence for me.

"I had sex with seven of Dan's friends last night." She stated it calmly, with a certain quiet pride, smiling as she said it. She looked at me as if she was checking to see if she had shocked me and was very happy that she had.

I didn't know what to say, so I said nothing as she patted her lip with her napkin, hopped off her stool, kissed me on the cheek, and walked out of the kitchen.

"I'm going to take a nap," she said as she left the room," I am sending you something." Then I heard the bedroom door slam and a few seconds later my phone sprang to life with incoming pictures, videos, and a text. All from Diane.

Enjoy

The pictures came up first. Diane and her cheerleader's outfit with various men. Diane partially in her cheerleader's outfit, with the same various men and others. Diane completely out of her cheerleader's outfit with the same men, many of whom were all in stages of undress. There were over a dozen pictures. Then, after having absorbed those body blows, I started clicking on the videos and watched those. There was sound and the ambient noises associated with exuberant sexual activity. As the action ensued, I noticed there was play by play and recognized it as Dan's voice. As I watched the multiple mini-movies and in those and in the pictures one thing was evident. Care had been taken to hide from view the faces of the male participants and equal care had been exercised in showing Diane's face. It was in every shot and every frame. Genitalia was also featured, theirs and hers. The men had been a diverse group, black men and white men had taken part. Dan had not wanted to be part of any lawsuits involving racial discrimination. Not that he would have had to worry. His legal representation would have been pro bono.

Having gone through each video multiple times and each picture more than that, I clicked out of that screen. I started to erase the pics and vids, but my cock twitched and stiffened against the satin fabric of my thong and my thumb couldn't push the button. I could not wipe away the evidence of her proud lust. The shame of it aroused me too much. Then, despite my excitement at having heard the maddening sound of Dan's voice and having seen what he got my wife to do, a moment of sanity overrode the delirium that watching the rampant sex had inspired and I scrolled through my contacts until I came across the number I had gleaned from Diane's phone.

Big Dan.

Then I found my sister-in-law's last incoming text. Then clicked . . . Share contact. With a single thumb stroke. I sent Dan's number to Dana, deciding to see if nature would take its course. Her response clicked in quickly.

Have you talked to her?

I replied:

Give me a bit. I'm about to. TTYL

Going into our room, my wife was sleeping the sleep of the dead and when I sat on the bed beside her, she stirred slightly and groaned softly. Having lived with her for over three years that was an indication to me that she was down for a while. Probably the night. Deciding this was my chance I went out onto the patio and called Dana.

Dana picked up and the first thing I asked was if Sean was still away. She confirmed he was.

"Call Dan," I told her after she answered my question.

"Now?" she asked.

"Tonight at least," I replied." Now is better. Diane's here, sleeping. Guaranteed he's horny." There was a pause on the phone. Dana was processing what I'd told her. She didn't know what had happened to her sister and I had no intention of telling her. I wanted to put Dana and Dan together and end this madness and my wife's involvement. Even if it meant throwing Dana to the wolves.

22

ONCE I GOT OFF THE PHONE, I went in and checked Diane again. She was out like a light. Her phone was on the nightstand, so, just in case, I took it with me when I left the room, placing it on the bar, near where she had been sitting earlier. After an extended drug and alcohol-induced sleep, he was likely to believe that she'd forgotten it.

IT WAS EARLY WEDNESDAY MORNING WHEN MY WIFE finally arose from the arms of Morpheus. Yawning and stretching and scratching in ways that made me want to offer to help. Without Dan, in residence, the thought had occurred to me to quietly slip into bed beside her. In the end, though, I went to sleep in the spare bedroom, partly because I knew nothing would come of being in such proximity to her naked body, but also because sleeping with my wife would prevent me from self-abuse. Having watched the videos and looked at the pictures of her Monday Night "touchdown dances" I was so excited that I beat off well into the morning hours.

"Coffee . . ." She cried to me plaintively as she shuffled into the kitchen wearing a pair of green pajama pants with little Santa's on them that I'd bought her at Christmas a couple of years earlier and a white Henley top that while showing off her breasts nicely also made obvious her numerous bruises. Diane plopped wearily onto the kitchen stool as I pushed a china mug of doctored coffee toward her. Before she noticed it, she happily discovered her phone on the counter under her nose. She was less happy to see upon checking her messages, what was not there.

"Shit," she exclaimed disgustedly as she slammed the phone down with a ferocity that made me think another trip to the store and another 1,500 dollars was in my future. She took a sip of coffee and burned her lip, which didn't help her humor.

"Trouble, princess?" I said it with only a slightly mocking tone as she coffee slopped out onto the granite. Well, more than slightly. She responded with a grunt, that I interpreted as an affirmation that yes there was trouble. I tried not to smile and mostly succeeded. Not totally, but luckily for me, she was too distraught to notice. Picking up her phone, she looked disgustedly at the screen and shook her head, after which she pulled herself off the stool with great effort and picked up her cup and headed back toward the bedroom.

"I need to get ready for the office," she called back to me over her shoulder." Can you make me breakfast honey? Please? As I'm sure you saw . . . I worked up a big appetite the other night."

The three-egg omelet I put together was a work of art. It was not received without comment, however, by my now profession-ally dressed and coiffed wife.

"Oh," she said expressing obvious disappointment.

"But I thought that was your favorite," I replied. It had cheese and mushrooms and spinach. No peppers. Those gave her heartburn, not unlike her recent escapades, which gave me heartburn.

"No," she said to clarify," It's just that I was hoping for pancakes." Then she flashed me an impish smile and added," Since Monday night I've been on protein overload. I wanted carbs to balance it out."

Disappointment aside, she attacked the egg creation like a rav-enous wolf.

"What," I said looking where the omelet had been, "you didn't lick the plate? I'm insulted."

She patted my arm tenderly.

"Oh, baby, don't be. I would have, but since Monday, my tongue is tired."

Patting her lips delicately with her napkin, she stood. She was barefoot, with her sensible business height heels on the floor beside her stool. Picking up the shoes, she handed them toward me.

"Please? "Asked using that seductive tone she always had when she wanted me to do something she knew I might not want to comply. I frowned at her and the shoes she was holding.

"Please sweetie," she asked again" If I bend over, I'll fall on my nose."

"Hmmph," I grunted." I'll bet you didn't say that Monday night."

Shaking my head and knelt and placed a shoe on each of her delicate feet.

Giggling Diane replied," Well no I didn't say it, but I fell on my nose a few times," then she kissed me lightly on the cheek and turned for the garage.

"Can you call my office honey?" She said as she walked away." Tell them I'm on my way."

23

Wednesday night Diane came home pouting.

"Dan's busy with a client," she whined as I took off her shoes and hurried to fix her a drink.

As I peeled the twist off a lemon I wondered if Dana was the "client" keeping Diane's boyfriend busy. I hoped so. Seeing my wife's bruised body, especially her battered pussy, I wondered given the newly available younger sister if Dan was taking the opportunity to "plow fresh ground." When I came back into our bedroom carrying the chilled vodka, Diane had stripped out of her conservative grey skirt suit. Her "lawyer clothes" as I called them. She stood in her bra and panties looking at herself in the full-length mirror. Then taking off the bra and then stepping out of the panties, she looked some more. So did I, marveling at how beautiful her body was even covered in bruises and bite marks. I was still staring as she took the drinks and sipped in a contemplative fashion closely regarding her reflected image. Turning, she looked at her butt, then her legs. Finally, she noticed me watching.

"Can you draw me a bath, honey?" She asked as she turned to get her robe from the closet. "While you're at it, I'll want another to drink in the bath. She handed me the empty glass as she said it. "Go on, be a sweety, and then we can have dinner."

Which we did, made by me of course, in the kitchen after Diane had lingered in her bath till the water had cooled and two more drinks had been consumed.

"Mm, this is great sweetie," she said eating hungrily. Beef stroganoff was one of Diane's favorites, and I took that into account when I planned the evening's menu. She alternated chasing bites of beef, noodles, and creamy sauce with large sips of pinot noir while checking her phone. She got into a rhythm of multitasking. Sustaining the body with food, the spirit with wine, and searching for some sign of "Big Dan" to maintain her libido. The look of increasing irritation as she looked at her fancy new device made it obvious the third quest was going badly.

"What's the matter, Puddin?" I asked, not being able to resist rubbing it in. Slowly, my wife lifted her head and as she did, she gave me a disgusted look. Her withering gaze caused me to drop my head and my sarcasm to cease.

After dinner, Diane took her wine to the living room, and I cleaned up.

"Honey," she called from the conversation pit," Let's watch a movie."

As I moved to join her, I heard her say, "bring more wine."

I did, and we sat together on the sectional. The same one on which she had sucked her lover's cock. The same one on which they had fucked like wild animals. Sitting together, in that desecrated spot, she pulled a fluffy throw blanket over both of us and flipped through channels, finally settling on an old movie we both liked. "Casablanca." I had lost count of how many times I'd seen it, but as it progressed it occurred to me, I was watching it with a different perspective. Was Laszlo the cuckold, or was it, Rick? Was Louie the Bull? Maybe he was fucking Ilse back in his office while her two cucks were busy opposing Nazis. Did she secretly want Major Strasser to beat her with his riding crop as her lover watched? After a while, the plane flew off and the credits rolled, and Diane got off the couch and hooked her phone to a cable on the TV. Then settling down under the blanket next to me, she clicked a button on the remote, and in scant seconds I was treated to the sight on my 65-inch flat-screen of my wife's face twisted in painful ecstasy as she was fucked doggie style by an enormous black man. Luckily, it was high definition, so I didn't miss the small saliva bubble she emitted as he pounded her pussy from behind. Then, I heard the same noises I had been hearing from my bedroom, only amplified courtesy of the modern miracle of surround sound. Next to me, Diane giggled which was mostly drowned out by her electronically enhanced cries of passion as she came in glorious technicolor in front of me larger than life, as the Black man climbed off, and was replaced by another smaller man, also black as the ebony giant who had assaulted my wife's pussy with such vigor walked around and, at Dan's spoken direction, she began to orally clean from his softening cock the juices produced by their coupling. As we watched, she moved closer to me, under the blanket, and she began to talk about each man, how he felt. How she felt as each fucked her. It was like a perverse play by play of a televised athletic event. A sexual Olympics, and as we watched and she spoke, with such enthusiasm about Monday's events, my angst began to fade, replaced by excitement. Fascination. Her most interesting comment came toward the end of the festivities, as the first man, the giant had once again become erect and moved behind her. As I plunged his fully engorged member into her sopping cunt, the Diane on the screen squealed, and the Diane, sitting beside me on the couch, in her jammies, under the fluffy throw said.

"He's so good with his cock!" There was amazement in her voice as she said it, and in the next statement, I thought maybe a little disdain.

"So much better than Dan."

Once the titillating, erotic disturbing images left the screen, Diane cuddled in close.

"Let's go to bed," she said with her nose buried in my shirt.

LET'S? I thought, more than a little shocked. As we got up off the couch, I was convinced she had misspoken and prepared to make my way to the spare room. Until as we got to the door, and I stopped and reached for the knob, and she took my hand.

"In here, silly," she coaxed me gently and I followed her in, where she waited as I turned back the covers of the fresh sheets, I had put there earlier that day. I stood waiting. She gave me a quizzical look.

"For God's sake, Jack," she said finally." Take off your pants and get in bed."

Without hesitation, I did, unceremoniously dropping trou and veritably leaping into bed to lay beside my wife for the first time since before the start of this ongoing debauchery. She lay on her side, and I lay on mine, and we looked at each other a long time smiling. Finally, she scooted closer and kissed me lightly on the lips. Then she took me in her arms and put her cheek against my face.

"Thank you for taking care of me," she said in a voice barely above a whisper. Her words hit me and, in many ways, made up for the words and actions that had recently inflicted so much pain. There was so much I wanted to say, but it all lodged in my throat in a big ball. Finally, I was able to croak.

"Always," I said, my voice very thick. Once I'd said it, she lifted her face and looked at me, her eyes seeming to fill.

"Do you love me?" She asked.

"Yes," I replied." I love you" The admission provoked a satisfied smile and a tight hug.

"Good," was her response and she pulled me to me, and my erection bumped her leg.

"Oooh," she cooed," someone is excited. Are you excited, honey?"

"Yes, babe," I told her, almost trembling with anticipation. She pushed herself away a bit as though to look at me more fully. Then, without saying a word, she turned onto her other side, away from me.

"Well, come hold me," she said." Then once I'm asleep feel free to go to the bathroom and . . . 'relieve' yourself.' Try to do it quietly, please. I need some sleep."

24

I AWOKE THE NEXT MORNING IN BED ALONE, but when I heard sounds coming from the master bath at least I knew where Diane was. I sat up in bed and watched as she came barreling out into the bedroom like an out-of-control eighteen-wheeler and headed for her closet. Where she noisily rooted around and swore till she found that which she sought, and she emerged triumphant carrying a heather grey skirt suit outfit still on its hangers. Placing the ensemble on a tall rack in the dressing area she began rooting around in her lingerie drawer until she brought out a pair of silk stockings. Then she threw off her robe and, standing naked she stood looking at herself in the full-length mirror. I looked at her too. The bruises and bite marks had already begun to fade from an angry purple to a more sedate shade of ochre. As she posed, I wondered if the fact that the thing I noticed were the consequences of Monday's sexual debauchery with multiple other men and not the more seductive qualities of her nudity represented the changing nature of our relationship. My wonderings were cut short when she spoke.

"Oh," she said sounding surprised," You're awake." Padding over to me barefoot and still naked, she leaned down and kissed me on the forehead, as her pendulous breasts dangled in my face invitingly.

"Be a dear," after she straightened and went back to the mirror," and make me some coffee."

Swinging my legs out of bed, I hurried to oblige. Unlike my wife, I was not naked. I was dressed in sleep pants and a Henley, not already prepared for the frigid winter still to come but to withstand her frigidity sleeping next to her in bed, a spot that had become unfamiliar territory. As I walked quickly out of the bedroom, she called after me.

"And one of those bagels," She said," The raisin ones? Light butter, please."

THE COFFEE WAS BREWED AND FIXED AS EXPECTED when I reentered the bedroom carrying Diane's favorite cup to find that she was dressed. Kind of dressed at least. She stood still looking at herself in the mirror but wearing smoke-colored hose held aloft by a black garter belt, something I didn't know she owned. What she was not wearing were panties or a bra. Taking the mug, she sipped and ignored me as she took the skirt off its hanger and stepped in, pulling it up to her waist and fastening it. The thing I noticed about it was its length. It didn't have any, coming down only enough to cover most of the tops of the stockings when she stood straight. If she bent at all, copious amounts of the lacy patterns peeked out in tantalizing fashion.

"Uh," I began, unsure as to how to say what I wanted to say." I didn't know you had anything quite so . . . short." She looked at me, smiled, and reached to the bottom of the skirt, and turned it so I could see.

"Hemming tape," she explained, as she smoothed the skirt back out and went back to her topless primping. "It's a miracle. I haven't used it since college, but it works wonders."

Wonders. Yes, it made me wonder what the other partners at her prestigious law firm would say when they saw it. Then, she put on her blouse, and as she buttoned it, I realized it barely contained her full breasts, and as she reached and rubbed her pert nipples that they showed through the dark, diaphanous fabric. Then, she stepped into a pair of shoes I hadn't seen before with heels taller than any other the other dozens of pairs she had. She was 5' 6" barefoot. In those shoes, she was at least six feet, and so taller than me by more than a few inches, a fact made very apparent when she stepped to where I stood in the doorway, getting close enough that her fulsome breasts brushed my cotton clad chest and she had to bend slightly to kiss me. On the lips, but in rather sisterly fashion.

"Thanks for the coffee, sweetheart," She said as she brushed past me." Is that bagel ready? I need to go. Busy day ahead. Busy, busy."

"YOU'RE HOME EARLY," I said AS Diane trudged into the kitchen, where I was finishing cleaning up from having made and eaten a late lunch. It was 2:15.

My wife slumped onto a kitchen stool and dropped her purse and shoulder bag to the tile floor while kicking off her overly high, high heels.

"Make me a drink," she said demandingly, then thinking the better of her tone added, "Please?"

Looking at her I decided to hazard a comment.

"Isn't it a little early to start drinking?" I asked. The withering look she gave me told me the comment was a mistake.

"I said, please," she reminded to, at which point I veritably vaulted toward the bar to be out of range of her laser like stare.

"Vodka?" I asked carefully. As I looked over, she shook her head.

"Do we have any of that shit you and Dan drink?" She asked, referring to the obscenely expensive Johnny Walker Blue Scotch which since the "dawn of Dan" had been harder and harder to keep in stock. My last trip to the liquor store involved a second mortgage on the house. We had three unopened bottles and I unscrewed the cap on one as I looked over and asked, tentatively, and asked how she wanted it.

"Straight up," was all she said as she continued slumping on her stool. So, pouring three fingers of the golden liquor I carried in the heavy cut-glass tumbler and placed it on the granite counter in front of her. I had water. Looking at my wife I knew one of us needed to stay sober and that it was going to have to be me.

"Bad day, Puddin?" I asked after she'd had time to ingest enough scotch to make the query safe. She had settled down a bit and she nodded, albeit a bit sadly, then began the story of her very short day.

"Dan took me to lunch," she said as she sipped more scotch." We were supposed to go back to his place after. But he had a client he had to meet." She held the empty tumbler out in a wordless demand for a refill. "Another fucking client," she said disgustedly. Taking the glass from me, she looked contemplative. "Plus, he looked kind of tired."

I listened without disclosing the fact that I knew the probable reason for her lover's fatigue. Not seeming to notice my silence or thinking it odd, she continued.

"Anyway, when he dropped me off at the office, David jumped my ass," she continued.

Given her choice of clothes that day, I could have guessed why, but I waited and allowed her to tell me herself.

"Why's that, sweety?" I asked trying for a naivete I had lost long before that afternoon.

She got a faraway look in her eyes and shook her head.

"Because he's a god damned, tight assed prude," she said sharply. She took another drink of scotch and continued her rant.

"Said I wasn't dressed in a professional manner!" She spits the words out as she said them, her eyes glowing angrily. "Hmmmphh!" She grunted indignantly and looking at her I had to admit she had a point. She was dressed professionally. It was just that the profession she was dressed for was not the legal profession, it was the one usually termed the "Oldest." For the sake of preserving my psychological and physical safety, I kept that opinion to myself, and she emptied her glass again. Taking it, I did the only thing a supportive husband could do in that situation. I got her a refill.

"Thank you, honey," she said sweetly as she took back her drink. Taking a drink, she then spoke again.

"He asked what had gotten into me," She giggled and pulled out her phone." I wanted to show him these." She pressed a button and a series of cock pics appeared in vivid 5G technology on the screen. Something I noticed was, the first several I recognized as Dan. The fact that I could recognize his "equipment" at that point was more disturbing than the fact that my wife had cock pictures in her phone that weren't me. As she scrolled through, I could see they were not all Dan. The sizes varied, (though all were larger than me), as did the ethnicities. Some glistened with her juices, others were poised to become so. The array finished and I looked away and back at her.

"You didn't," I said. She once again looked at me like I was stupid.

"NO!" She declared firmly, then a smile snuck across her beautiful though overly made-up face. "But I wanted to." She emptied her glass yet again and placed it down. Getting up off her stool, she headed to the hall in the direction of our bedroom, leaving her shoes, her purse, and her shoulder tote abandoned on the kitchen floor for me to rescue.

"He told me to get myself pulled together," she said as she made her exit "The first step I'm taking in that process is a nap." Turning as she left, she blew me a kiss.

"Thanks for the drinks, baby," With that, she left me to once again, clean up her mess.

AT TEN TILL SIX THAT SAME EVENING, I was watching the evening news when a text came in from Diane.

Can you draw me a bath, please . . .?

Naptime was over, and I hurried to comply, eagerly anticipating another Dan less night together on the couch, cuddling and watching movies. When I entered the bedroom, she was laying on the bed naked sleepily stretching her limbs out seductively. As soon as I stepped in that stopped and she clutched the sheet to her breasts, covering herself from my view, as though denying that I was allowed to see her nude. She seemed embarrassed. So, I walked past as casually as my prurient nature would allow and went into the master bath.

"Can you use the bath bomb I love?" She asked. "The lavender?" She specified though it was harder to hear over the sound of splashing water. I checked the temp. Perfect. It was a whirlpool tub and once it was filled to the desired level, I started the jets and she appeared in her fluffy white robe.

"Thanks, hon," she said, effectively dismissing me. "Oh, and can you bring me another drink for the bath . . . please?"

So, I did and luckily enough (for her) the churning, bubbling water kept her naked body safe from the intrusion of my view. After taking the glass I handed her, she smiled in a benevolent fashion that told me wordlessly, "Go away."

So, I did, checking the fridge and larder to see what I had to make a proper dinner. After careful consideration is decided on lamb chops and was letting them marinate when another text came in from my darling bride.

Come help me, please.

Leaving the lambchops to their own devices, I scurried back to the bathroom, hoping to get . . . what? A glimpse of breast? A hint of buttock? Sadly, though once I got there, she was out, in her robe, with a towel around her head.

"Would you like me to get you your jammies?" I asked solicitously. She shook her head.

"I need to get dressed," she replied. "I'm going out."

The response left me crestfallen as she rushed past to the vanity sink.

"Here," she directed, "Come dry my hair while I do my makeup. Hurry now."

So, I did, getting her heir dried and brushed so it fell softly on her shoulders. Then, she even showed me how to apply polish to her fingers and toes, which I didn't do badly considering it was my first time. When I was done, all her nails were shiny and bright red.

She looked at them and smiled after they had dried. She did not admire them for too long as she jumped up and went to her closet. When she came out, she was carrying scraps of fabrics and small scraps at that. She then finally doffed her robe and stood before me stark naked, though she quickly stepped into one of the garments, which it turned out were shorts. Accent on the short part. When she had pulled them up as high as they would go on her hips, (which wasn't very high), they dissected the round moons of her buttocks and rode up exposing a large portion of each cheek in the process. She was looking in the mirror and turned this way and that, finally turning her butt to the glass and peeking over her shoulder. Then, she reached back but didn't tug the shorts down to cover herself more. She pulled them up to further reveal more of her luscious bottom. That was the moment where I understood a man could drool and cringe simultaneously. The shorts were white, the material thin and very tight.

Then, she squeezed into the outfit's top. A tube top, similarly, tight and made of a thin stretchy material that when on, his little and exposed much of her magnificent breasts, including her prominent nipples and puffy areolas. She shimmied to get the placement on her torso just right, then she stepped into a pair of shoes that, like so much of what she wore recently, I'd never seen. Platform heels. I had seen them, a long time ago in Vegas, at a strip club, a group of us had wandered into while attending a convention of insurance executives. As tall as the six-inch heels had made her, the platforms gave her another three inches of height. They were open-toed and so showed off my paint job brilliantly.

"Can you do the buckle, Jack?" She asked. So, I knelt before her and did the shoes' straps. The position was seeming more natural the more I was in it.

She stood before me, a 6 foot 3 large, busted goddess, then she went to the closet and came back with a white full-length fur coat that I knew she had, and I'd never seen her wear. It was real fur. Ermine and no longer "politically correct" to wear out in public, but wherever she was going, political correctness seemed not to be a consideration. Certainly, her wardrobe reflected that sentiment. She posed before the mirror and posed. Turning this way and that looking at herself over her shoulder, coat open and closed, then after several minutes seemed to pronounce it good. She went to her bureau, rummaged through her drawer, and came out with a white clutch bag and looking at me asked, "Where's my purse?" I had brought it into the bedroom after picking it up from where she had abandoned it on the kitchen floor. She transferred various articles into the smaller bag, and then put in her phone, closed it, and looked at me.

"Can you call me an Uber honey?" She said it as though she was asking, but the tone was more a demand. I clicked the app on my phone and after five minutes of silence that was only awkward on my part, the car was out front.

"Don't wait up," she advised as she strode out of the house, but being reasonably sure of where she was headed, I couldn't promise I could sleep. I knew however what I had to do. Picking up my phone again, I clicked the speed dial to call Dana and warn her hell was on the way.

27

IT WAS 3 A.M. BEFORE I GOT EITHER DAN OR DANA TO ANSWER. They obviously weren't ones to allow modern technology to interfere with sexual excess, but finally, I got through, though what Dana told me was not what I'd expected.

"No," she said, "Diane didn't show up. Why should she?" She seemed genuinely perplexed, which made me suspect that Dan had literally fucked her brains out. That might have explained my wife's recent behavior.

"Yes, I was at Dan's all evening," she explained. "Just us. He had dinner brought in. Lovely. I only wish Sean wasn't coming home later this morning." She sighed, "Husbands are so inconvenient."

Wives can be too, I thought to myself, when you never know where they are. It was 3:07 a.m. and mostly I knew where Diane was not. She wasn't at Dan's, and she wasn't home. Simple, I would eliminate places she wasn't, and I would eventually know where the hell she was. Shouldn't take more than two to three years.

Or a couple of minutes, as I heard a key turn in the lock of the front door and wrapped in her full length politically incorrect fur, in walked my wife. I sat at the bar sipping a scotch as I watched her saunter in smiling.

"Have you had a nice night?" she asked after she kissed me on the cheek.

I nodded and said, "It was all right. Want a drink?" She shook her head in response and turned to walk away.

"No thanks. I need to get some sleep. I have fences to mend with David tomorrow." Then she looked at her phone and laughed. "Or maybe today."

She went to the bedroom, and I followed. Once she was in the room, she opened her coat, under which she was stark naked. She carried the fur to her closet and carefully hung it and came back out clad on only her platform heels. As I looked at her feet specifically her ankle, I noticed something else. It was like a necklace but on her leg. It glittered in the ambient light, and I knew it was an anklet and that anklets were part of Hot wife lore. The outward symbol a married woman was ready and available. A statement to the world. She saw me staring at it and smiled broadly.

"Like it?" She asked. I nodded wordlessly and she continued. "Dan got it for me," she said. I hadn't worn it since he gave it to me, but somehow, tonight, it seemed appropriate.

Appropriate was the last thing it was, but propriety seemed to have gone out the window since our Hot wifeing saga began.

Then, having kicked off her shoes and yet still wearing her new adornment my wife climbed into bed. She threw back the covers on my side and patted the mattress.

"Get in here mister, and hold your wife," she said cheerily So, I dropped the sleep pants I'd put on as I waited the night before, and still in my boxers and a Henley, I got next to Diane, under the clean sheets I'd changed earlier the previous day. As I got close and placed my head on the pillow, I detected something besides the scent of laundry detergent and fabric softener. Diane was covered in the smells of sex. Distinctly male smells. Like those of Dan but different. Sweat and cologne and semen all mingled on her body, and the aromas made me wonder, as I lay there. I knew where she had not been, but not where she had been. I knew what she had done, but not with whom. Then a strange and conflicting thought entered my fevered brain. Was my wife cheating on her bull?

28

I WAS VACUUMING WHEN DIANE CALLED AT LUNCHTIME. It was something she had done a lot B.D. (Before Dan) but had not as of late.

"David and I made up," she informed me. "I'm the golden child again."

"Kissed and made up?" I asked, unable to resist the question.

"Ewww," she said, "No. He is definitely not my type."

Though amusing, the comment was slightly disturbing in that David had always reminded me of me. Same age, similar height. Greying hair. Similar builds. Boring executives with bored wives. Did his wife have another man waiting in the bullpen? I hoped I never found out. I should call him and advise him to get her some golf lessons.

"So," I began cautiously. "Will you be having dinner here tonight?" May as well let the elephant into the room and let the poor thing play a bit.

"Yes . . ." she said it hesitantly as though checking her messages for a better offer.

"Will Dan be with us?" I was going to have to drag every detail out of her.

"Yes . . ." Again, as though she thought so but was not sure.

There was a pause and I thought she was done with me, and I got ready to say goodbye. However, as usual, I was wrong.

"Do you have dinner planned already?" She asked, to which I informed her, no, but there were several options in the fridge and freezer.

"Hmmm," I heard her respond. "Do this," she began, "can you call him? To ask what he'd like?"

My mind was reeling. Did she know I had checked her phone? Did she know I'd found his contact information? Pushing the panic I felt down deep inside me, I struggled to be calm. The strategy I decided to use was one that had been working well for me recently. I played dumb.

"I would love to sweety," I replied nervously, "But I don't have Dan's number." Having said it, I knew it would provoke a response if she knew the truth. Luckily, it did not, and she did not.

"Yes, Jack I know," she told me impatiently. "I'm sending it to you now."

She bought it. I could breathe again, as the message with her lover's info came in. Looking at it, it matched what I already had, so I hit delete.

"I will call him immediately," I said, happily relieved.

"Good!" There was an edge to her response. Not happy so much as satisfied?

"I have something special planned for tonight. Everything has to perfect."

"It will be," I told her, finding it hard to disguise my disappointment. The nights with Dana had obviously not had the effect I'd hoped, nor had Diane having sex with another man. My wife and her bull were on the makeup trail, which meant I'd be trailing behind them eating dust.

"Goodie," she said sounding more pleased. "Thanks, Jackie. Look I have a client in five. Talk later?"

"Yes," I replied. "We definitely will."

Then I heard a kissing sound over the cellular connection, after which I heard, "Love you."

My wife hadn't said that in quite some time, and I was surprised, albeit pleasantly so.

I responded, "Love you too," after which the phone went dead, and I wondered to myself, what the fuck was going on?

29

B Y, 6:30 P.M. WHEN DAN ARRIVED, we had talked, and I had established his preferences and a beef Wellington was cooking in its pastry shell. Diane had come home an hour early with shopping bags full of fresh, unspoiled, and sexy lingerie and a new dress. Seeing that she was so early and had departed the office even earlier made me wonder if she and David HAD kissed when they made up. Did tongue make up for lost work time? Life had become a continual mystery. Despite my confusion, I met him at the door, dressed as directed by my wife. Black slacks and dress shoes polished to a high shine. White broadcloth dress shirt, and a black-tie, in a Windsor knot. Full Windsor which was more formal but which a lot of guys can't tie. I could, having tied it every weekday for decades, I had gained the skill. As bad as I was with my cock, I was good with ties. Though when I greeted him at the door, Dan didn't seem impressed.

"Good evening, Sir," I said with as much feigned respect as I could muster while acting like a servant in my own home. "Please come in Sir." He removed his topcoat and handed it to me once he was inside.

"Where is Diane?" he asked pointedly. So much for pleasantries.

"Miss Diane is still upstairs getting ready for you Sir," I replied, being as overly polite as she had instructed. I hung his coat in the hall closet as I explained. "She asked me to get you seated in the living room and get you a drink. Scotch?" Leading him to the couch, he sat in the spot where he had debauched my wife the most. It was my assumption that was his favorite place. Once I was sure he was comfortable, I departed for his drink.

"Light ice, remember," he called after me.

"Yes Sir," I answered, assuring him he had been heard.

As I moved around the bar and then took Dan his drink, I mimicked the behaviors of every well-trained maître' d who had ever served me in the best restaurants in which I had dined and drank. Once he had tasted the Scotch and light ice and nodded his approval, I stepped unobtrusively off to the side. As I stood, I straightened my tie self-consciously, secretly happy to be dressed as I was. Given the turn things had taken, I'd been afraid my wardrobe for the night would be a French maid's outfit. Diane allayed my fears, telling me I "didn't have the legs for it." I was simultaneously relieved and a little insulted since I thought I had pretty, nice legs. The hat though . . . that would have been another matter.

Finally, my musings were interrupted by my wife's grand entrance. Diane was always stunning. That night she was more so, in a slinky, skintight, lowcut red dress. Long, but split up the side all the way to her waist. The color perfectly matched her toes and fingernails.

She went quickly to Dan and kissed him, passionately. Obviously aroused, he insinuated his hand under her dress. Into the deep split to what I knew to be her pantiless, depilated cunt. She giggled naughtily and looked at me then back at her lover.

"I'd like a drink," she said. Though why she was asking him rather than telling me was perplexing.

"Vodka," he barked in my direction. "Straight up, with a twist."

I hurried to meet my wife's alcohol needs. What Dan was too busily groping to notice was Diane's sly smile and encouraging head nod toward me before I left the scene.

Upon my return, the big man had made further progress and one hand was burrowed deep under my wife's dress and the other was fondling her right breast. He'd had to put his drink down to accomplish it, but a guys gotta have priorities and his were always defiling the woman I loved.

As I handed her the glass, she pushed his hands away.

"Slow down, lover," she cautioned. "A girl needs refreshment." She took a big sip, though sip was too weak a term for the draining she did of what I'd given her. Reaching down, she picked up Dan's glass and pushed it toward him.

"Drink up baby," she said, "You're falling behind." Then she looked at me again and arched her eyebrows.

"I am sure dinner's almost ready, isn't it Jake?"

"Yes dear," I replied agreeably and rushed to the kitchen to fulfill that promise.

IN NOT TOO LONG A TIME, THE MEAL WAS SERVED to the happy couple, with me as their waiter. Once the last bite was consumed Dan rose from the table and dragged Diane toward the bedroom for "dessert." I began to clean up but when I looked toward them as they were beating a hasty retreat, my wife motioned to me to follow. I hesitated. Obviously, this time I would be included in some way. The ways I was being included had not yet made me very happy. But she motioned to me again before she disappeared into our boudoir, so I went after them. Not fully understanding, but I was starting to get used to that.

Once I reached the bedroom, Dan had begun, once again, to paw relentlessly at Diane's sleek form. She made it obvious she wanted him to stop, but about the time I was about to step in (for all the good I might have done), she looked at me, shook her head, and pushed him away.

"Honey," he told him seductively, "I want this to be special. I want to put on a show for you. Don't you want my special show?" His answer was a definitive yes.

"Good," she declared, smiling broadly. "Now, let me take care of you." Then, she looked deep into his eyes and said, "Will you let me take care of you?" This time it was him who nodded after which, she slowly, and carefully removed his clothes until he was naked. She drew him close, and kissed him hard, and reached down and stroked his impressive erection and looking at him, licked her lips.

"Now," she told him. "It's my turn. Come over here, where you can watch the show."

Having said that she carefully steered him toward the corner. Where she sat him down in the chair.

My chair.

Once he was seated, she climbed onto the bed, still in the red dress and heels, and slowly, and sensuously, did a striptease as he stared. His arousal grew to untold heights. His breath quickened. His cock stiffened. Until she was naked except for the red high heeled shoes. Then, she got off the bed and strutted toward where her Bull sat. She settled herself onto him and ground onto his erection. He tried reaching for her which she stopped and wagging an index finger at him said, "Not yet." Then she continued her erotic dance until she kissed him again, and once the kiss broke off, she wrapped her arms around her massive torso and held him until I heard . . .

CLICK and *CLICK*

Dan heard it too and tried to pull his arms away. However, he could not, as the cold steel of the handcuffs my wife had trapped him in held him tight. Diane, meanwhile, jumped off the chair, leaving the big man alone, naked and restrained as I watched, perplexed, and amazed.

Opening the drawer of the nightstand on her side she got her phone and punched several buttons, and setting it aside, looked at Dan again. He looked back. Both their eyes were on fire and not with the sexual arousal I'd gotten used to seeing.

"What the fuck, Diane?" He asked. He pulled at the cuffed and they rattled against the strong oak chair frame and clattered like Marley's ghost.

Laughing she shook her head.

"You cheater . . . you fucking cheater!" She shouted at him.

Confronted unexpectedly by the awkward truth Dan struggled, not with his bonds, but with thinly veiled denials. Denials are hard to present when a man's naked and cuffed to a straight-backed chair. Especially when confronted by an ill-tempered, vengeful woman. She slapped his face. Hard.

"With my sister?" she said angrily. "My sister! Who does that?"

"Let me explain . . ." was the last thing Dan said before we all heard the front doorbell ring. My wife looked at me and smiled.

"Answer it," she said turning to smirk at her captive. "We will wait here."

THERE WAS A MAN AT THE DOOR. The first thing I noticed was his size. He was big. Blot out the sun big, (except it was night). The other thing I noticed was he was African American. So many strange things had occurred in the last few weeks that a huge black man coming to the door of my suburban house late at night seemed normal. So, much so that all I could think to do was greet him.

"Good evening," I said, not knowing what else to say.

"Good evening to you," he replied smiling pleasantly. "I'm here to see Diane."

Of course.

"Come on in," I responded as I opened the door wider and stepped out of his way.

"I'm Eugene," the man said as he entered, and he held his hand out. "You must be Jack."

We shook hands and I nodded.

"Who else would want to be?" I joked. Well, I was kind of joking. As I started down the hall toward the bedroom, I explained, "Diane's in here." As we walked down the hall, Eugene engaged in small talk.

"Nice home you have here," he said then explained he lived not far from us in an area noted for expensive, upscale homes. As he spoke, I merely nodded. I was numb.

He entered the bedroom ahead of me. My wife smiled when she saw him and they embraced, while Dan cried out in confusion. "Gene!" The ebony giant looked at the naked man like he was a bug.

"It's Eugene, motherfucker," he spit the words out at the man who no longer was my wife's bull. Then Eugene turned back to Diane. Holding her at arm's length, he looked at her.

"Those bruises and bites are healing up nicely," he observed, to which my wife giggled.

"You added a couple more last night," she replied. Eugene shook his head and grinned.

"I'll try to be more careful in the future," he said apologetically.

"You'd better not," she responded teasingly.

"You wear them well," he said back to them then asked, "Shall we?"

Reaching for his belt buckle, she said "We shall." He then turned toward me and said, "You, okay?" The question startled and slightly embarrassed me, but I recovered from the lack of a slight quickly.

"Please," I told him, "Be my guest."

Diane had his pants down and was in the process of getting his cock out when Eugene replied, "I guess I already am."

She looked at his dick hungrily. He was well endowed, but not in the stereotypical BBC way. He was slightly smaller than Dan, but it just looked different. Dark and uncircumcised with large balls. It was an impressive package and made my wife lick her lips. Then, before she dove in, looked over at the naked man she had bound in the corner, on my chair.

"Last night," she said, "While you were fucking my sister, I was fucking Eugene, which is what I am going to do again now. But this time, you get to watch." She took the black hardened member between her lips and sucked it several seconds and she could wait no longer. Pulling away, she lay back on the bed and spread her legs, inviting him in, before launching another brief verbal assault.

"And, you know what watching makes you, right, Dan? Hmmmmm? Sure, you do." Eugene was chuckling as he knelt on the bed and aimed his cock for my wife's sopping pussy.

"It makes you a cuckold, Danny boy. A fucking cuckold. In the cuckold chair. I put a set of horns on you. Do you feel 'em, honey?" When she said it, I reached up reflexively to rub my own head and I heard Diane moan, Eugene groan, and Dan wail in despair and anger. Eugene penetrated her and they coupled savagely and for a very long time. Shaking the bed, shaking the room, shaking the walls, and shaking Dan so entirely that he finally slumped lifelessly in the chair. He was defeated.

Diane and Eugene lay there a while as I watched, still stunned, and awed by what happened. Then, Eugene climbed off my wife, stepped off the bed, and got dressed. Once he had his shorts and pants back on, he bent toward her and kissed her lightly on the lips.

"It's been fun," he told her quietly, then looking at Dan, said, "Want me to stay till you turn him loose?" Diane shook her head.

"Jack and I can handle him," she said confidently.

He straightened and took two steps to where I stood and towering over me, reached his hand to me.

"Jack," he said politely, "Thank you for the hospitality."

We shook hands. "You are welcome," I replied, unsure as to how to respond. It must have been right because he smiled and patted my shoulder before he turned back to my wife.

"Are you two free next weekend?" he asked, "Gayle's at her mothers in Wichita."

"Sounds great," she replied. "Jack's an excellent cook."

That news made the big man smile and with that, he bid us adieu as I showed him to the door where we said our polite goodbyes, after which he climbed into his Mercedes sedan and drove away at a reasonable pace.

Back in the bedroom, Diane was staring daggers at her former lover, and he was looking back pleadingly.

"How soon are we letting him loose?" I asked. The question made her laugh.

"Can't be soon enough for me," she replied. Then she grabbed my shirt front and dragged me to her and kissed me with a passion greater than that with which she had recently kissed any of her bulls.

"I love you, you know," she stated it as fact, and in looking into her eyes, despite all the recent evidence to the contrary, I believed it to be true.

Then she grinned mischievously, jumped up said, "Let's get this asshole out of here and you can help me clean up. Then we can go to bed. Who knows . . .?" She winked. "This might be your lucky night."

AND INDEED, IT WAS, THOUGH HER DEFINITION OF "LUCKY" was a hand job, but it felt good to achieve an orgasm that wasn't "do it yourself." Once I cleaned myself up, we lay in bed holding each other close under the sheets that smelled like Eugene.

Dan had left with only mild rancor. He seemed tough, but at heart, he was a whiny, little bitch and he dressed and slinked away to avoid further humiliation. So, we lay in our room alone, in a way we hadn't been in a very long time. Without the specter of "The Bull" hanging over us.

"Do you like Eugene?" She asked. Thinking about it, I replied honestly that I did.

"He was part of the Monday Night Football group," She explained. "I met him there and we hit it off. Even if Dan hadn't double-crossed me with Dana, I was planning to call him."

Once again, she had given me the chance to exhibit my newest superpower, playing dumb.

"So," I began cautiously, "Dan was having an affair with Dana?"

"A two-night stand," she said, "it would have been more. He was playing me."

"Strange thing was," she continued slyly, "How did she get his contact info? Sneaky, little bitch."

I shuddered slightly, knowing she knew. Diane laughed.

"We've told you before," she said, "Dana and I tell each other everything."

Then, she hugged me tight.

"I know why you did it," she continued. "The gangbang scared you. Wanna know a secret? It scared me too. Even though I didn't show it." She hugged me tight. "You were protecting me. I love you for that." Craning her neck up, we kissed again, then she settled her head back onto my chest.

"I love you," she said flatly, "For so many reasons. Everything else is just sex."

Then, she pulled the covers up around us and snuggled closer.

"Speaking of which," she said suppressing a soft yawn "Donald's coming over next Monday night. You'll like him too. Nice man, with a big cock." She emphasized the big theatrically. It had the desired effect as my previously spent cock began to find new life.

"A guy named Nate will be here Tuesday night. We are meeting him for drinks at Costas' then bringing him back here. Then we have Bradley Thursday and Eugene starting Friday to spend the weekend."

As I lay holding my wife in our bed, overwhelmed by what she'd just told me, one thing had caught my attention.

"What about Wednesday?" I asked

Diane raised up slightly and kissed me on the nose, before rolling onto her other side and grinding her ass into my growing erection.

"Silly goose," she said sleepily," Even a cuckoldress needs some rest."

ABOUT THE AUTHOR

John Stone is a typical midwestern man with a fascination and a love of powerful women. He has given up his mundane nine-to-five existence to live to dreams and write about them. These are their stories.